Beautiful Flower

Beautiful
Flower

A. L. Reynolds

Beautiful Flower

First published in the United States of America
by A. L. Reynolds

Copyright © A. L. Reynolds 2013

ISBN 978-0-9900206-0-8

This book is a work of fiction. Names characters and incidents are
either a product of the author's imagination or are used fictitiously.
Any resemblance to actual people living or dead, or to any events,
is entirely coincidental.

This book is dedicated to:

Sellaci & Simir
You gave me strength to overcome my most
challenging obstacle, fear of failure.

You are my love, my pillar,
my reason to "stop running".

Chapter 1

My friend Chase and I have been going out together to Koko's, the singles club, for five years now. Chase is twenty-nine, and can only be described as a flamboyant, high-maintenance homosexual who loves to shake his moneymaker every Friday night. For some reason, he drags me along with him each week.

He's a bartender at a popular hotel hot spot and goes to college part-time. He's more intelligent than he might seem at first glance, and no matter what sort of lonely mood I'm in, I always enjoy hanging out with him. Occasionally, when he's misbehaving in one of his favorite way, I call him Thurston, which is his first name. He was never too thrilled about taking his father's name, and he'd smack a bitch if they teased him about it. Hell, I've seen him do it.

As for me, I'm Zuria Ayanna Johnston. I'm thirty-four, and in serious need of some love. At this point, it would be nice to have handholding and roses for no reason, but I wouldn't turn down someone willing to push me up against a wall and take me on some sweltering afternoon. Suffice to say, it's been a long, strange journey to find Mr. Right, and I've apparently still got miles to go. Sometimes it feels like playing GI Jane... *"Operation failed to apprehend subject!"*

Growing up in the harsh streets of Atlanta with an African father and an African-American mother taught me how to survive on my own. I can still hear my mother's incessant reminder; *"Be independent!"*

My folks met two years before I was born. My father was actually my mother's doctor, and she was a waitress working the night shifts at a corner diner. Just like in the movies, according to them, they instantly fell in love. Some days they saved a quarter, other days a few dollars, and sometimes nothing at all, but they eventually tucked away enough to get the big house, the three cars, the indoor pool, and their very own Johnston's Medical Center. They didn't want their children living in their footsteps, which led them through the dangerous road of the Civil Rights Movement, so they worked together and always stuck to their plan. More importantly, they both taught us to be proud of who we were and where we came from.

I've always been known as a "good girl", with the reputation of never falling into bed with a man unless I thought he was "the one". That may have been somewhat true, but after a while, a woman's gotta let her guard down and live a little! Hell, it's been three months since I gave up eating snacks and sweets, and I know I look good. *I don't have time for nonsense*, I constantly tell myself. I'm pushing thirty-five and my clock is ticking louder every month. I may be independent, but I'm also a proud black woman without a man to give me what I need.

My ex-boyfriend and I decided to go our separate ways after four long years of turmoil. The fighting and bickering may have worn my patience down, but the biggest problem was that he wouldn't commit.

Manuel Cartagena is a thirty-seven year old Puerto Rican and African American mixed man, born and raised in Manhattan. He's 6'4", polite when he wants to be, but he usually chooses to go with arrogant. He's a licensed Construction Contractor, so as you can imagine, he's built like a man is supposed to be built, and is ruggedly sexy. We met when he came through Georgia on a business trip, and we kept in touch with each other on the phone, through emails, and even short visits. Within a year of our back and forth flirtation, he decided to move to Atlanta to settle down with me. I was ecstatic.

He started to show his true colors less than six months into our little domestic setup; he disrespected me, looked at other women, and generally seemed disappointed with his choice to move. He wasn't the only one. I gave him plenty of chances to change his chauvinistic attitude, but a dog will always be a dog, no matter what you dress him up in.

There was no doubt in my mind that he wasn't the one for me, but I tried to be patient with him because he was all I had. Well, four years and thousands of tears later, I finally stood up for myself and ended it. Thanks for wasting my time, asshole!

I called and told Chase that I'd meet him at KoKo's tonight. We usually take turns driving, so one of us can drink, but I wasn't feeling too well tonight and told him to go without me. Even though I tried to bow out, we are like two inseparable peas in a pod, so Chase begged me to show up for at least an hour.

"Zuria, you've gotta show up. If you don't, I'll be depressed!" he said. I could practically hear him pouting over the phone.

"Don't be so dramatic. I'll see you later, ok?" I said.

"Girl, if you don't take some damn Tums and bring your crazy ass out here, I'll come over and drag you here!" he half-joked.

"Give me an hour, Chase. I'll be there. Will that be enough time for you to pound a few shots of chill the fuck out?"

"Do you promise?"

"I promise on Manuel's future grave! Alright? Jesus..."

Chase giggled at the seriousness of my tone and answered gleefully, "Alright, girl. I love you!"

"God, you sound tipsy already. Love you too...you drunk."

"I heard that!"

"Ciao!"

"Later!"

I walked around my apartment in my pantyhose and robe, then plopped down on the sofa to drink my cup of Herbal Ginger Tea.

Maybe the new tea would make me feel better. I didn't want to miss out on a night out; I know how crazy Chase and our friends can be after a non-stop week of work. Once Friday night hits, they love to look good and make sure everyone knows it. And what if my "poetic lover" is there? My new friend, Amir, is the proud owner of that nickname, at least when I'm thinking about him on stage at Poetry Slam nights. He has some mad love for poetry, and is remarkably talented. He's like a different person once he gets behind that microphone...

The tea helped, and thinking of Amir put me into a better mood. I decided to get dressed, but nothing too fancy. I only promised Chase that I'd show up, not be the belle of the ball, and I doubted I would stay for more than an hour.

I threw on my black halter-top dress and stilettos. Simple, short, and sexy enough. I took one final look in the hallway mirror to check my makeup and goddess-braided hairstyle, and then put on my gold earring hoops that practically hung down to my collarbone. I grabbed my long leather jacket and purse on the hall table before stepping outside into the sultry swagger of another warm Friday night.

***

I walked into Koko's and saw Chase bouncing in his seat and snapping his fingers to the beat of a techno remix. He was surrounded in a round booth by a wild pack of old high school friends and random acquaintances.

As expected, they were in typical end of the week high spirits, talking over one another and laughing louder than any other group; they weren't hard to spot.

Chase's jaw dropped as I approached the table. He looked shocked and more than a little tipsy. His glazed hazel contacts swimming in a sea of bloodshot streaks are a dead giveaway. It looked like he'd been hanging out with Rastafarians again.

"Damn, Zuria you are sizzling tonight!" Chase praised as he sipped on an Apple Martini and nodded at a fine milk chocolate man smirking at him from the bar.

"Why, thank you kindly! You're a sight for sore eyes, sugah," I said, returning the compliment.

He shooed someone out of the booth, wrapped me up in a hug and motioned me to sit down. "After you, darlin."

"Such a gentleman tonight, Mr. Chase!" I said.

"Call me C-licious!" he suggested. Everyone in the booth laughed and nudged each other, smirking at Chase's usual over the top behavior.

Laughter is the best cure for anything. Chase and I have told each other the most scandalous secrets over the phone, and laughed until we cried. Secrets you would be ashamed to tell your mama, and secrets that could break up happy homes. I grinned at him, already glad that I came, and sat down, nodding to those people around the table that I knew.

After a few more drinks, Chase started to feel frisky. He leaped up without warning and headed for the dance floor. I knew he'd be calling me to come join him within moments. I would do the usual and ignore him for a while as I sipped away at my virgin Pina Colada and smile at his promiscuous little ass waggling to the music. He'd never been the type to keep up with the freshest dance moves, but he always looked good doing...whatever he wanted to call it.

Chase is truly one of a kind, and one of his best assets has always been sense of humor. He would crack up a funeral if it got too boring for him. The only thing I can't stand is when he comes to visit and always goes through my shit. He thinks my bedroom is like a second closet, and my makeup, accessories, and clothes are never safe. I've never let anyone wear my personal items, not even my only sister. However, Chase is practically my adopted sister, so I split the difference and let him use my lip balms, lotions, and clear nail polish, like a puppy getting a treat.

Chase usually thinks he's more of a woman than me, but I bring his ass right back to reality when I tell him, "You can carry tampons all you want, honey, but until you can use them, you're still a man in my book." We fight about stupid shit all the time, but it's always out of love, and our friendship is certainly never boring. We have a lot of love between us, as though he really is related to me.

After a few more cocktails, everyone with breath in their body and shoes on their feet are on the rainbow-lit dance floor. I started to feel that urge as well, so I shuffled over along with everyone else, and began moving my feet and hips to the pounding beat. The dance floor was packed with bodies, and the hot, Atlanta night had made its way into the club. Sweat poured down my face, and ran into my eyes. I closed them and let the rhythm take control of my body. I could feel the bass in my chest and a seductive, sexy voice begged, "Just a little bit longer, baby," as the tune ran through my head over and over.

As the song reached its climax, I felt firm, yet gentle, hands on my waist. It seemed like a familiar touch, but I was enjoying the song, and didn't want to open my eyes to find some drooling beast of a man staring back at me. I opened them wide enough to read the soundless movement of Chase's mouth saying, "Sweetie, tuuurn around!" I did, slowly, and heaven help me, it was Amir. Now, the likelihood of someone stepping up to me with chronic halitosis and dive bar pick-up lines is slim, but who knows what could happen any given Friday in the club.

Amir is thirty-two with smooth cocoa skin. He's always clean-shaven and smelling like he just stepped out of a tropical shower. With his sweet cherry lips and infectious smile, he's one of the finer men in town. He's originally from London, England, but at the tender age of ten, his mother wed an American Photographer, which is how they ended up in Georgia. His biological father abandoned him and his mother when he was only five years old.

While adapting to his new home, a world away from London, he developed an interest in his step-dad's work. He started entering modeling competitions for fun with his stepfather's help. It quickly turned into more than a weekend hobby once he and his family realized how damn good-looking he was. He never looked back; Amir had been a male fashion model since he was twelve.

I'd known Amir for about four months. I met him at the Friday Poetry Slam at Sage's Jazz Café after watching him perform. Even though I wasn't a huge poetry fan, I fell for his unique way with words, and that smile didn't hurt either. After he finished, I went out of my way to talk to him, and I found that his power over words didn't stop at the edge of the stage. We saw one another a few times after that, and we'd end up discussing the current status of poverty and violence in urban versus non-urban communities, or the foreign policy of America and The United Kingdom. He loved politics, and stimulating debates; I felt smarter every time we spoke.

Once I knew that it was Amir, we stared into each other's eyes while swaying lightly from side to side; a slower song had taken over the speakers. We weren't doing any particular dance, just admiring each other, but it somehow wasn't awkward. Honestly, his smile was always enough for me. It turned me on faster than any ass grinding that we could have done to a different song. I'd have liked to stick my tongue into his ear and whisper something like, "Bring your toothbrush?" But I tried not to be so forward with Amir. I didn't want him to think that I was just some freak who needs a good lay, although the second half of that might have been true.

Amir always knew exactly how to move. For a relatively slow song, I was barely keeping up as he slipped and glided around my body, gently moving and guiding me with a touch here and a tug there. "You know I love a man who takes control, but don't think for a second that you can show me up on the dance floor," I said to him while pulling off a few slick moves I hadn't done in years. Amir smiled and busted out a quick sidestep that dropped him to his knees in front of me with his hands cupped gently under my ass. I felt my temperature rising, and a surge of wetness slip onto my thighs; my nipples tingled, but his hands were nowhere near them.

While he was kneeling down South smelling the sweet nectar of a real Georgia peach, he kissed me on the space below my belly button. Then, he slowly moved his way back up my body, sliding his body along every inch of mine. Seductively, he slowly laid his lips on my forehead and held onto my waist as he said, "Sweet…tender… Ayanna." Ayanna is Swahili for beautiful flower; it's also my middle name. For the record, that was the night I fell in love.

I'd never felt such compassion for any man as I did for Amir, and it had been growing since that first night at the Poetry Slam. Even with Manuel, to whom I must have said, "I love you" a thousand times over those four years, my soul never felt as connected as it did with Amir. Before that, I didn't know whether I believed in soul mates, but sweet visions of love, trust, and security flooded my mind when I thought of that man. I may have had problems with falling in and out of love, but not anymore. I remind myself of that every day.

Before reaching "maturity", I used to fall for the same old bullshit and cheap lines that every young woman experienced at some point in her life. Of course, the sex was great, particularly before I knew how good it could actually get, but having an intelligent conversation afterwards while still damp and intertwined with your lover...that was quite a bit harder to find. I wanted to convince those panty-sniffing, loin-burning assholes that I was someone special. Instead, I had just been another gullible girl on the block. Luckily, nothing lasts forever.

Chapter 2

After saying my goodbyes to Chase and the growing crowd of good-looking men near him, I was hoping to be alone with Amir for the rest of the night. The look in both of our eyes confirmed that we were both feeling the same way, so we strolled down the sidewalk, hand in hand. It felt bizarre to hold hands in public with someone I actually cared about; I had the funny sensation that I was in middle school again, holding hands with my crush in the hallway between classes. Amir didn't seem to mind, although Manuel had always pulled back, saying that it felt too awkward. He was always finding reasons not avoid any public display of affection. Looking back at the long list of his issues, that one seemed pretty small; maybe he just didn't want his *hoes* to find out he had a girlfriend.

Amir and I walked out into the muggy night towards my car, which was closer to the club. His car was parked at the other end of the huge parking lot, so I insisted on giving him a short ride over there.

We agreed that he'd follow me back to my place. I gave him one small kiss on the cheek, letting my lips linger, as his had done on my forehead. That seemed to satisfy him. The closer I got to my apartment, the more I began second-guessing how I wanted to play it with Amir. I didn't want to scare him away by coming on too strong, but it might be impossible to withhold my feelings for him much longer.

I searched in my mind, weighing the pros and cons. We had a lot in common, even knowing most of each other's likes and dislikes, passions and pet peeves. He's single, and has no children, just like me. No matter how much my defensive mechanisms tried to keep me safe, all I could think about were his eyes, and the smell of his skin mixed with sweat on the dance floor...for the moment, it didn't take much to convince myself that Amir was the man for me. Either way, if it didn't turn into a relationship, at least I knew that we would remain good friends. Well, good "friends with benefits". Hopefully.

As we walked into my studio apartment, I mumbled something about my feet being sore from dancing so much in my newly purchased stilettos. Amir gestured that I should keep them on *just a little bit longer.* Before I could even put the kettle on, he laid his hands on my shoulders, spun my body to face him, and lifted me up with breathtaking force. *Damn, he's strong!* I quickly wrapped my legs around his waist and my arms slipped down around his neck. I didn't want this foolish, yet gorgeous, man to drop me; I don't wear a size two anymore, you know? Either way, I was ready for him to set my world on fire; I was a tinderbox and he had a lit match dangling from his fingers.

He pushed me up against the dining room wall, rattling the mounted wine rack, and slipped his hands up the sides of my thighs. In one movement, he tore off my pantyhose and dropped them behind him. I held onto his shoulders while kissing his face and latching onto his well-muscled back. His hands continued to work my dress up around my hips, and after a few minutes, he released his manhood from his black silk boxers and rubbed it up and down my already damp clitoris. His full, succulent lips pressed against mine with such passion and ferocity that I moaned uncontrollably. My moans melted into screams of pleasure as he slid inside me, then began moving deeper and deeper with every thrust. My eyes flamed with passion, but my mouth was paralyzed.

All it could do was tremble like a newborn baby crying out for its mother's teat. *I must tell him how much I want him to stay...stay with me for eternity,* I begged with my almond eyes. I couldn't resist the urge to claw his back slightly as I clung on to him in ecstasy. "Ouch!" Amir screeched playfully. He looked at me with a serious expression, but couldn't hold it, and we both burst out laughing.

I could tell that Amir was turned on by my aggression; he smacked his hands under my firm behind and squeezed my plump, tender buttocks together. He continued to push his sweating body against me, utilizing the strength of his toes and flexing his calves with every surge of energy. We shifted from having sex to making love while sliding slowly down the berry-wine wall until we felt the coldness of the freshly waxed pine on our bare skin. Amir's shirt buttons littered the floor, evidence of my animalistic desire for this man. He stayed inside of me, even as we sat crumpled and tangled on the floor. He had broken out into a sweat and I was drenched in the fever of sex.

Rhythmically, I began revolving my hips in long and short thrusts as he grabbed a mouthful of my bouncing breasts. Our hearts were beating like drums in an African ritual, and we did seem primal in that moment, wild and free. My knees begged me to collapse from strain, but I wanted to make sure that he would never forget his first time with me.

***

One hour, thirty minutes and five seconds later, I relaxed in the enfolding comfort of his arms and enjoyed the crisp, clean scent all round me.

The air in the bathroom, which is where our passion had dragged us, dripped with a combination of sweet pea, mountain rain, and the thick odor of sex and sweat.

I gently massaged his chest and kissed the side of his ribcage as my "poetic lover" began to fade and doze into dreams. I could even hear a light snore creeping out, but as always, he seemed to read my mind, so he shook himself awake and wiped the corners of his mouth, smirking at me. *"Well, you certainly repaired my plumbing problem tonight,"* I thought. I took one final look at Amir's lasting grin and drifted into a deeper sleep than I'd had in weeks.

***

The sun crept in through the bamboo blinds, and my first thought as my eyes fluttered open were of Amir. I had hoped to see that beautiful sculpture of a man lying next to me, so my heart dropped after I turned over and found myself alone in bed. I started to panic; *here we go again,* I thought, as I reached for my red satin robe, which was hanging on the headboard post on his side of the bed. I heard the crinkle of paper beneath the sheet as I leaned across the place where I had last seen Amir. I pulled back the sheets and found a freshly cut rose lying across the pillow.

I picked it up, along with the slightly creased note written in beautiful, curving script. *"Good morning, my beautiful flower! I hope last night was as spectacular for you as it was for me. This flower seemed a fitting thing to give the beautiful person blossoming in my life. Red was an obvious choice; I believe that's the color of love, right? Zuria, please forgive me for not saying goodbye this morning. I'm hoping to see you again tonight. Love, Amir."*

I was speechless as I reread it for a second time, and then a third. What could possibly be the reason for such a touching note? Am I just a blossoming friend? Was he telling me that he loves me? Or that he is *in* love with me? Some people can't tell the difference, I had learned that the hard way. I just couldn't understand how our subtle flirtation over a few months turned a corner and then love was being discussed in notes left on pillowcases. I pressed my nose into the soft, velvet petals of the rose and tried to understand how I could be so lucky. What does a model want with a plain Jane like me?

I'm a Guidance Counselor with a one night a week social life, but I guess Amir saw something in me that drew him closer. It always made my heart pound and my thighs quiver when he would look right in my eyes and compliment me on my "radiant smile" or "divine curves". That man could work his words, but maybe it was only a physical attraction for him. But according to him, I could "keep up a house", am an awesome cook and a hard-worker as well.

I aimlessly walked around my apartment, asking myself all of these questions and debating silently in my head. I pushed play on a new reggae CD I'd bought that week; reggae always slowed me down when things get too hectic. After the beat of the first track picked up, I scanned the case to find out who had produced the song; it was off the chain! Sli-Pro, huh? Well, he definitely knows what he's doing; his beat made me want to take a vacation. At least, take a vacation with a certain poetry-loving model.

I laid my head back down on my pillow as I reached for Amir's. I pressed my face into it and breathed to the bottom of my lungs, trying to inhale whatever he left behind. I slid his pillow between my legs and squeezed it, remembering how the man with that same scent had been between my legs less than eight hours earlier. I continued to daydream and tried to come to some conclusion about the letter he wrote me. I was still baffled by why he left without saying goodbye. Maybe he felt guilty and wanted to avoid facing the conversation this morning, but then why would he leave the note? Admittedly, it would have been a little strange waking up beside someone other than Manuel after a night of steaming hot passion, but all things change. Also, Amir had been amazing, gentle, giving, and ridiculously sexy. As much as Manuel was somewhat fresh in my mind, I had always believed that timing was everything, so I went for it. As, I remembered, for the record, I gave just as good as I got!

I laid naked beneath my sheets, reveling in the smell of sex that still surrounded me. Questions wouldn't stop racing through my mind. What does he expect from me? Am I ready for love again? If so, are the feelings mutual?

Smooth-talking, "sensitive" men like Amir had played me in the past, but something felt decidedly different about this chiseled, mind-blowing man in my life now. *That's what you always think...* The cynical side of my conscience can be a bitch sometimes.

In my heart, I knew that Amir's goal wasn't to get into my pants and split. We'd been taking our flirtatious friendship pretty slow for a couple of months now, so if he was waiting to hit it and quit it, his attention probably would have turned a long time ago. Given our normal interaction, I doubt that Amir had expected anything more than a PG-13 show the night before; you know, a few dirty words, maybe an unhooked bra. I hoped that it hadn't surprised him too much when I threw this sweet divine love of mine on his dark and sexy behind! I needed it; he wanted it. Case closed.

I know that there are times when Amir is bored out of his mind, especially when I discuss shopping, makeup, or Chase's latest lovers. Despite that, he's always very attentive. If I have dumb jokes to tell him, he's there to laugh. If I want to vent, he talks me through it and builds me back up. The signs were right in front of me, but I was too busy protecting my heart. Maybe he has felt this way for a while, and was waiting for the right moment. Maybe he is *in* love with me. Maybe...maybe...oh hell, maybe I shouldn't think so damn much!

He loves me! He loves me not! Slowly, I picked away at his rose like a puppy love struck girl again and hoped I knew what I was getting myself into. I decided to save the petals for my bathtub, which Amir would hopefully end up in. I wanted to bathe that smooth, caramel skin and give him my own budding flower to savor.

I would also tell him that I love him too.

Chapter 3

Another week was securely in the books and Saturday had arrived. Saturday was always my favorite day of the week; I had planned for my usual pampering from head to toe. I had been working hard all week, and I'd gotten worked hard the night before too; my feet were in serious need of a pedicure. Once I arrived, the deluxe spa package was just too tempting to turn down so I settled in for a morning of luxury.

Chase says that I'm too frugal, and while that is sometimes true, it really depends on what I'm shopping for; a girl's got to have her priorities. Usually, when it comes to my body, I don't spoil myself too much.

I think my last pedicure was two months ago, and I had a massage sometime last spring. That Saturday, I decided to break out of that shell. The world needed to get ready for the rebirth of Zuria, Queen of Ethiopia. Well, maybe I wasn't a real queen, but I sure knew how to make myself feel like one; it started with a head to toe day of beauty.

Sometimes, I have flashbacks of the cute little games I used to play with my sister, Nadia. We'd play dress up while mother was out enjoying her "me" time in the garden. I'd sneak to my mother's closet to find the gold dress with the diamond accents on them and rummage through the dozens of fancy hats. I loved finding the African-patterned hats and trying them on in front of her large, oval mirror.

I don't think I'll ever forget those shoes. As far as I could remember, my mother never had a scuffed shoe in her life. All of them were shined and meticulously lined in rows in her huge, walk-in closet. Nadia and I knew they were off limits, but we'd test my mother's patience, not to mention her duration in the garden, and swish our behinds down the hallway in them like miniature shoe models on a catwalk.

It was always an adventure going in that closet! Sometimes, we'd sit and play in there for hours, until our mother would run through the house in a frantic rage. We'd hear her yelling, *"Girls, where are you?"* over and over, getting louder as she came upstairs.

Every parent knows that when the house gets suspiciously quiet, the children are most likely doing something mischievous or they've fallen asleep in some unexpected place. That rule didn't apply to my sister and me; we'd just get lost entertaining one another without getting into any mischief beyond wrinkling a few dresses.

I miss my sister; she passed away last year. Nadia contracted AIDS from her husband who had conveniently forgotten to mention that he had spent time in prison before they met. He had been too ashamed to tell her that three men had stripped him of his manhood and dignity. She got pregnant, but due to the virus, the child hadn't survived. My sister was only twenty-nine when she passed away.

Chase, with his perpetually perfect timing, called as I was finishing my last treatment. My beautification process was complete. I paid the Nail Technician and gave her a generous tip. Chase was launching into a long explanation about some young guy he had met the night before, so interrupted him, told him I'd call him back, and made an appointment for the next weekend; I didn't feel like getting a massage today, but next Saturday promised another slice of freedom. I left the Fancy Feet Spa and Salon, feeling ready to face the world, toes out.

I had an extra skip in my step for some reason, possibly because of the downright freaky moves Amir and I had put on each other the previous night. Nothing to be ashamed of there - that man has some moves! It had been one hell of a good night and I was looking forward to more of the same that night.

I got back on the phone with Chase and discussed the wonderful time we'd had at KoKo's.

"Girl, don't you know I couldn't keep my hands off that chocolate brotha?" he said, laughing hysterically.

"Oh baby, I know. I sat there and watched you work your magic," I said.

"Yeah? Did you learn anything? You know C-licious could teach a course in getting a man!" he joked.

"I learned not to have more than two drinks in one night," I replied.

"You've got some jokes today, lady. What's up with your sassy mood? Does it have anything to do with the rest of last night, Miss 'Leaving with Mr. Poetry'?" he asked.

"That may have a little something to do with it. But I wanna hear more about you and that fine young beau of yours.

You certainly worked it on the dance floor with your sexy diva self!" I teased.

Chase had ended up dancing with the guy he had been eyeing most of the night. The guy finally read the signals and asked him to dance. One dance turned into two; two dances turned into all night. Chase is so handsome I wonder how any man resists him. Shit, if he weren't gay, I'd be on him in a heartbeat. Of course, I wouldn't want to ruin one of the best friendships I'd ever had though.

"You hungry? How about Cougar's Bay for lunch," he suggested.

"Alright. Is one o'clock cool with you, babe?" I asked.

"Sure! Girl, we have some serious talking to do!"

"Why? What do you mean?"

"It can wait 'til lunch, Sugah Plum."

I had an hour to shop and get my clothes from the cleaners, since I didn't want to come all the way back after lunch. Conveniently, I wanted to pick up a new perfume I'd been dying to wear. I already had enough bottles to open a boutique, so I didn't actually need to add anything else to my collection, but there was something irresistible about putting a brand new scent on your body.

I moved as quickly as I could through the stores, knowing that if I didn't, I'd be in trouble! The credit card monster would come out, as usual, and I would mysteriously lose control of my common sense. I found the perfume, paid in cash, and was on my way. "Better luck next time, Lacy's!" I giggled, as I left the department store with only one small bag.

I hadn't taken two steps before I spotted Manuel sitting on the hood of his brand new blue BMW, sipping on what was probably a Caramel Latte, his standard.

"When did you get back?" I asked carelessly, as disinterestedly as I could manage without being rude. Manuel took his sweet time before answering, and took the pause to check out my body, smirking. I could see this conversation getting very ugly, very fast, so I openly looked at my watch and waited impatiently for him to speak.

"Been back for a couple of days now, Zuria."

"Alright. Well...nice seeing you. Take care." I said, and turned to walk away.

"Slow down, baby. Aren't you going to ask about my trip?"

"Wasn't planning on it. I'm in kind of a hurry."

"I'll just have to tell you anyways, now won't I?" Manuel smirked.

"Manuel, maybe some other time. I'm having lunch with a friend." I began to get annoyed, and looked at my watch again, hoping he would get the hint.

"With who? That maricón, Chase?" he said as he took another calm sip of his Latte.

"What did you say?"

"Maybe not. In that case, who's the lucky bastard?"

"Damn it, Manuel! How about some respect for my friends?"

"That depends who it is. Do I know him?"

"Listen up, Pendejo! First of all, you can't just pop into my life and try to tell me what to do or who to do it with, comprende? It's over between us! You had your chance, and you blew it. End of story. You're too late!"

"Liiinda, please listen to me," Manuel begged with his strange version of sincerity as he reached out to grab my arm. Linda means pretty in Spanish. "On my business trip, I couldn't get you off my mind. Most guys wouldn't admit this, but I'm man enough to tell you..." He paused briefly as a flash of guilt spread across his face. He seemed to be telling me the truth. "I wake up in tears sometimes when I think of how things ended. Don't you know that I'll always love you, Zuria?"

Tears started to creep into the corners of my eyes. I'm fighting with all my might to keep Manuel from thinking that he's breaking through to me.

I couldn't believe what I was hearing, so I stared at the ground, the car, anything but his face. I just folded my arms and got lost in space. I thought about my night with Amir and what would happen if I fell for Manuel's bullshit yet again. I quickly came back to my senses. That would have been my third time on his emotional rollercoaster; I refused to go along for another pitiful ride.

"Manuel, I've had enough! I'm not going through this again. I'm not putting my heart on a platter for you to tear it apart again! I'm looking for someone to love me for who I am. Hate to tell you, but you're not that someone" I finished with pride.

He didn't seem surprised at my speech, just angry. "Is it that poetic little pretty boy bitch? Amir Townsend? Damn, you didn't waste any time!"

"That's none of your damn business, Manuel! If you had kept your genes in your jeans, we wouldn't be standing here now would we?" I shouted back.

I looked at my watch again; ten minutes had passed. I only had five minutes to get to Cougar's before Chase would start to worry. He knows that I'm punctual when it comes to my work, family and friends. I decided to end the conversation, with or without his permission. I started to walk away, keeping one eye on Manuel to make sure he didn't try anything crazy. Our eyes met locked as if we were fighting a battle that no one else could see. Manuel looked away and stood shaking his head, like he'd already been defeated.

Chapter 4

I stepped into the cool air-conditioned interior of Cougar's Bay, a popular steak restaurant where my friends and I occasionally went to unwind after work. Most of the tables were empty and the atmosphere was calm, just what I needed. I knew that I probably looked as emotionally drained as I felt, so much for my refreshing morning at the spa. I told myself all the way to the restaurant that I wouldn't let Manuel ruin the rest of my day, but our encounter was hard to block out. I wanted him out of my memory. We could never be just friends; it would have been impossible. We'd been through hell and back as lovers, multiple times. At a certain point, it's best to just leave well enough alone.

I walked around the piano bar towards the back of the restaurant and found Chase waiting for me, flipping through a menu.

"Sorry for being late. Hope you weren't worried," I told him, trying to seem normal. My acting skills don't work on someone as perceptive as Chase; he immediately knew something was wrong.

"Zuria, you okay, sweetheart? Why are you late? Why such a long face? Did someone do something to you?"

"One question at a time, hun. Did you order?"

"No. Screw the food. I'm more concerned about the tears sitting in your eyes." By this time, he looked ready to jump out of his seat. "Now, who did what? I'll cut 'em, baby. You tell me where to go."

"Chase, chill out. Nobody hurt me. Don't go worryin' your sweet self about that, alright? I just bumped into an old friend while I was shopping," I said as I took off my coat and placed it over the seat next to me.

From the look on my face, he could guess which old friend.

"Manuel? What did that no good, egotistical, Spanish-speaking piece of shit want? Did he think he could come up into your business and sweep you off your feet the way his cheating ass did the first two times? No fuckin' way! Over my dead body!" Chase said as he channeled his energy into flipping the pages of his menu and writhing around in his chair, as if Manuel was going to pop out from behind me looking for a fight.

Gently, I grabbed his arm and waited for him to look into my eyes and calm down. I always asked him not to act so ghetto, especially in some of the nicer places we went to. I knew we'd end up in jail as soon as he heard any lip from these snob-ass rich folks and decided to shut their mouths the hard way.

"Manuel just wants to ruin my chances of finding a new man...that's all he cares about. He doesn't really love me. He's just being selfish and doesn't want any other man dipping into his stash. We both know that Manuel's capable of being a good guy. He just doesn't want to grow up, move on, and focus on something new, that's all."

The server arrived to take our order. Chase already knew what he wanted. I scanned their new list quickly, not wanting to make him wait, or come back in "just a minute", which would be ten. I wasn't in the mood for eating; what I could use was a drink. *Damn, Manuel knows how to wind me up. I should just get something light. Aw hell, forget that!* I thought, deciding on my meal suddenly.

"I'd like a sweet tea, a steak burger, a side salad, and a bowl of fresh fruit instead of fries," I told the server.

Rarely do I eat meat, but Cougar's Bay was tempting the hell out of my stomach. Besides, I'd been doing well on my diet, only cheating a couple times a week.

Chase checked out the server before ordering his usual. "Well hello there! Look at you...looking all divalicious! Sweetie, I'd like a Cougar's Bay steak sandwich, with all the fixins, steak fries, a side salad and a slice of key lime pie."

How one person could put away so much food at one time and still manage to fit in those jeans I will never know. That man is the definition of carnivore. He'd fight his mother over a half slab.

"And, what would you like to drink Sir?" the server said sweetly, clearly amused by Chase's forward, casual way of speaking.

"Diet Coke," Chase replied. He grabbed the cloth napkin from his lap and discreetly patted the perspiration from his forehead. It doesn't take him very long to get heated over me; he had always been like an overprotective brother to me.

Moments later, Chase had to take an important phone call and stepped outside. I looked around the room to see if there was anyone I knew; I didn't want anyone to see me looking upset or to have heard any of our conversation. People love to talk, and they would make up any old story, whether or not they knew the facts. While staring at a young couple giving each other short kisses over their desserts, I drifted off, thinking about Manuel. *God, I hope he didn't follow me.* That was the kind of shit he use to do time we were dating. He would be sitting somewhere inconspicuous reading every word on my lips; he was the one sneaking around with other women, yet he never trusted me.

Chase returned to the table and wiped his cell phone screen with a napkin. He took another deep breath, as though settling himself to tell me whatever that mysterious...something that he told me was on his mind.

Chase has always had honest eyes; he would never lie to me. He gathered himself, looked at me, and started talking.

"Baby, yesterday, I saw Manuel and he wanted me to talk to you...to put some sense in your head. I told him that you were a stubborn woman and that I wouldn't be able to change your mind, even if I wanted to. That's what I wanted to tell you, honey." He had said it all in one breath, like he'd been physically holding it in since yesterday.

He reached out for both of my hands and held them gently.

"Please, don't fall for his shit, baby girl. He's a thug. You're a beautiful woman and can have any man you want. You don't need some selfish punk."

"Thanks for saying that, but if that were true, I'd be kissing on Larenz's chest right now," I said, puckering my lips into the air, laughing.

"I just need some time to clear my head. I do have a vacation coming up soon. Maybe we can go to St. Thomas or Dominica or something," I suggested.

"Ooh, that sounds goooood. Give me the dates and the place, I'll be there."

"Why not? Let's do the damn thing, we both could use a break from this city."

"Child, you see how easy it is to get back to your old self again? That's what I like about you, Zuria. You need to keep your mind straight and drop that old baggage for good. Don't worry yourself about some man! There're too many fish in the sea. You just gotta learn to throw back the guppies," Chase declared dramatically.

"I know, Chase. It's just easier said than done sometimes," I concurred.

I'd grown accustomed to how Chase looks at life and relationships. I knew I'd never have to worry about him hurting me or taking our friendship for granted.

He was basically everything I wanted in a man, except for the liking women part, but that's fine with me. I'm certainly not on Mother Earth to judge anyone. Who am I to tell someone who to love?

My cell phone vibrated in my coat, and I quickly answered it. *God, please let it be Amir!*

"Hello, Zuria speaking!"

"Hey there, beautiful! Do you have a sec?" It was Amir, thankfully.

"Of course, what's up?"

"I was hoping I could come by around six or so tonight, does that work?"

"How about 6:30?"

"Perfect. Oh, and baby, I'm sorry for not being there to see your flawless face get out of bed this morning. Hope you didn't take it the wrong way. I had a few things I had to take care of today, but I barely had you off my mind for a minute. Forgive me?"

"Amir, no need to apologize. Honestly, I understand."

"Well, I'll make it up to you tonight. Promise. Call me if you need anything specific...I know how some women are," Amir chuckled.

"I think I'm covered," I replied, a slow smile spreading across my face.

"Well then, until later, mon chéri."

"Ciao."

"Ciao."

I hung up and saw Chase smirking at me with one hand resting under his chin.

"Have you been listening the whole time?" I asked him, raising an eyebrow.

"Of course not. I was just admiring that pretty smile you've got all over your face."

Chapter 5

I was unpacking all the items from the supermarket that I needed for dinner that night when I noticed a new message on my answering machine. I pressed play as I started washing and chopping some vegetables.

"Hey Zuria, it's Amir. Hope you haven't changed your mind about tonight, I'm looking forward to seeing you. Call me on my cell if you need me; I'll be at the gym for a couple hours. Talk to ya soon!"

I was in the mood for some slow R & B, so I pressed play and got lost in Kelly's mellow voice. That man sure knows how to make a sistah yearn for good lovin'. Every time he hit those high notes, I'd wrinkle up my face and break it down like a diva with stomach cramps. When I was alone, I'd usually sing into my remote control, or in this case, my vegetable knife, pretending like I was center stage.

I decided to return the call before I forgot. *Pssh, as if I would forget to call Amir. Hell, I could crack my head, get amnesia, and still pick up the phone.* I have a silly habit of talking to myself, either out loud or in my head. Amir and Chase both love to tease me about it...they think it's cute.

His husky, sexy voice answered the call. I didn't speak at first; I just wanted to hear him say my name again.

"Hello. Hello. Zuria?"

"Hey, Amir! How are things?"

"Good, thanks," he replied, breathing deeply into the phone. It reminded me of how he sounded last night.

"Just letting you know that I'm more than ready for tonight. I'm actually preparing tonight's gourmet meal as we speak. Chef Zuria Johnston is in the house this evening," I said proudly.

"Well, I'm just getting off the treadmill. All I've gotta do is wash up and head over there. That alright?"

"I suppose so...I'll be waiting here impatiently. Don't be too long now, love," I said in my terrible British accent. He laughed to himself, and it purred in his throat. Delicious.

We said our goodbyes and I continued dancing and singing into my knife as I cut the spinach for the salad. The turkey breasts were marinating in olive oil, fresh herbs and spices. The California Blend veggies and rice pilaf were in their own pots ready to be steamed. I had to do some quick cleaning, pick out a sarong and hair wrap, and take another shower. By then, Amir would be knocking at the door.

I like Amir so much that it never bothered me if he showed up at my doorstep unannounced. He had never shown any signs of being the jealous type, which is a huge turn on for me. Of course, I don't give him a reason to be. I just tell him, "Anytime...day or night!" The thing is, you don't have to give some men a reason to be jealous. Too many of them are just manipulative, insecure little boys.

A number of years ago, I dated this bi-racial guy named Jacob who was obsessed with where I was, whom I was with, and what I was doing. He wanted to choose my friends, change the way I talked, and have approval over the way I dressed. I kicked his ass to the curb in a month. My father was pleased, to say the least. He couldn't stand being around Jacob.

The problem is, my father is very old fashioned, so he'd prefer that I marry a black man. According to him, if Jacob's father is Italian and his mother is African American, he's not actually "black". I told him that was ridiculous, but it didn't matter. Jacob failed all of my father's other tests as well. On the other hand, my mother told me that if you have one drop of black blood in your body, then you're black. No one outside of our race will care how white you look if there's African blood running through your veins.

They both had their own opinions and I respected them growing up. My father agreed to respect my feelings and allowed me to date Jacob without interfering. It wasn't that he hated Jacob because he wasn't black; he just didn't trust him. Over the years, I learned that my father was pretty good judge of character.

I took a few minutes to relax and threw myself on my bed. Manuel crossed my mind for a split second. This afternoon's run-in still had me wound up. There was no way I would allow him to mess this up with Amir and I. He had to learn that I was no longer in his life, and figure out a way to move past it. I couldn't imagine why he'd go to Chase for help after all the nasty things he'd said about him while we were dating! Of course, I knew not to be surprised by anything Manuel did. He was one of the most manipulative people I'd ever met.

As I turned over on my side, still steaming about Manuel's silly stunt, I heard the doorbell ring. I almost broke my ankle jumping over my cat, Scribbles. I call him that because he looks like he's scribbling something important on the carpet when he scratches it. Who knows what goes on in that cat's head...I did a quick final check of myself as I headed for the door. I also took a fast look over everything else. My crib was spotless. Dinner was ready and smelled divine. My heart was beating faster than normal; it had been a long time since a man could make me nervous on the other side of the door! I took a breath and collected myself as I opened the door for Amir.

I greeted him with a big smile, although inside I wanted to purr like Scribbles. Amir was dressed in a matching P. Farm shirt, blue jeans, and white sneakers. He smelled like Jamaican Musk, which was perfect on a natural man like Amir! He was holding a bottle of champagne, a stunning bunch of red roses and a shopping bag.

"Welcome back; mi casa es su casa."

"Good to be back!" Amir paused as he stepped in and gave me a long, slow kiss by the door. "Damn, I've been waiting all day for that."

"You're not the only one," I said as I took the roses he held out to me. I thanked him, especially for the flowers, as he carried the grocery bag to the kitchen counter.

"What did you bring me this time, Amir?" I teased, playfully.

"Well, I know how much you love fruit, so I bought some fresh strawberries dipped in white chocolate."

"Oh, sweetie, you're too good to me! We might have to eat these in the Jacuzzi..." I said as I winked and strutted my behind a little more than usual over to the refrigerator to put away the fruit.

I don't think I ever smile as much as I do around him. Just having him in the room is intoxicating. Not only that, I was completely comfortable around him, even though he could make my heart race with a single glance.

I could dance like crazy with my friends, sing obnoxiously, play video games, scratch my bum, and put my elbows on the dining room table without a single judgment or snide remark. I was waiting for him to show his true colors too, but he was always the perfect gentleman.

That's why I usually give a man a few months before I let him take me to bed; I want to see what he's really like while he waits for it. If he starts finding reasons why he can't hang out as often or keeps "missing" my phone calls, he's probably just getting what he really wanted from me with some other woman.

I always believed that there were a few good men waiting for a woman like me to come along. I'd learned to make sure that he was more interested in my mind than my body. When a man can wrap you up in good conversation and appreciates being around a real woman because of how she makes him think...then it might be time to surprise him and let him in for the good stuff.

The table was already set for dinner, so I took out the hot pans from the oven and set them out while he poured some wine. There was nothing too formal about our dinner. We just popped in a hip-hop album and started eating. I remember watching Amir unconsciously bob his head back and forth; somehow it was hilarious and sexy at the same time. After he caught me staring for a third time, I smiled and bobbed my head around too, pursing my lips at him. It was so casual with Amir, so easy to have fun, even when we weren't trying. I was so hungry that I forgot all about my diet and devoured my meal. Amir didn't feel any shame in doing the same thing. I'm not gonna lie, I'm a pretty good cook when I have a reason to be.

"Zuria, that was absolutely delicious. You manage to satisfy me every time. The question is, do I get breakfast too?" Amir said with a grin after he wiped his mouth with his napkin and drained the last puddle of white wine from his glass.

"Sorry Amir, dinner was free; you have to earn your breakfast," I replied with a coy grin.

As I remember, Amir had only slept over at my crib three times, including the night before. On the other two occasions, we had cuddled on the sofa and talked until dawn. We'd actually never had breakfast together, because we had slept until late afternoon on those days.

We put our empty dishes aside, sipped hot ginger tea and enjoyed the easy conversation and the laughter.

"Well, I've got to say, I really enjoy every moment that we spend together. No one has ever made me feel so complete," said Amir.

"I feel the same way, Amir. I can tell that you actually mean it; I appreciate hearing the truth," I said, staring into his soft, brown eyes.

"I *do* mean it. And I always tell you the truth," Amir said as he stood up and walked over to my side.

He reached for both of my hands and continued.

"Zuria, I love you. You even make me smile in my sleep. When I wake up in the morning, an image of you in my mind is far more glorious than sunshine."

Now, that would sound like bullshit if it were coming out of someone else's mouth. However, that is never the case with Amir; he always knows what to say to make me melt, and he never says shit he doesn't actually believe.

"I... I... lo-...I'm, I'm...speechless! I'm sorry, Amir," I said, feeling ashamed. I couldn't let those three words roll off my tongue unless I was completely sure it was the right move at the right time.

"Shhh... it's ok, Zuria," Amir said as he placed his soft, index finger on my lips as a sign that everything was absolutely fine. "I understand that you want to take it slow, and that's fine. But we both know that last night changed things; we're in a new chapter now. Hell, we might be in a new book."

I took a few seconds to think about what Amir had said and realized that it made perfect sense, as always. The thing to do was to keep moving forward and hope for a long-term relationship. If I wasn't ready for a big step, I simply had to tell him that I didn't feel the same way and end it right there and right then.

"We are, aren't we? I just need more time to sort out my thoughts. You shook up my brain pretty hard last night." I said as I dropped my head. What I really wanted to tell him was that I needed more time to lick my wounds. Manuel has certainly made it difficult for the next guy.

I have always given more than I received, especially when it came to relationships. I gave Manuel everything I had without holding anything back. My mother always told me never to let my guard down completely. "Don't love anyone more than you love yourself," she always said. I should have listened, but instead, I paid a high price when things with Manuel crumbled.

After that, it became difficult for me to say three simple words to an amazing man that had the potential to give me as much as I gave to him.

There have been times in my life when I couldn't tell the difference between love and lust. When I was a young, naïve college girl, I believed every man when they said, "*I Love You*". For the next few weeks, he made me feel special, as though I was the only one. However, too often I only ended up being his little secret. I was never good enough for him to take out on a date or be formally introduced to his friends. I found out the hard way that it wasn't love after all. Each time, I was devastated, particularly since I thought I was being careful.

Doubt swallowed me until I could barely breathe; the memories of my past were surging and messing with my mind. I took a few more sips of the tea and counted calmly in my head, a technique I always used when I got upset.

"Are you alright? Come on...sit down on the sofa," Amir said.

"No, really...I'm fine. I'm just happy that you're here," I said, holding back some brimming tears. I didn't want him to think I was some basket case on the verge of a nervous break down. I knew that I had a strange habit of getting lost in the space of my thoughts; I had to work on that.

"Give me those pretty feet. Let me take all that pain in your eyes away," Amir said. He began to rub my feet as I lay back on the sofa. He's always been so gentle and patient with me. I was thankful that he'd stuck by my side as a loyal friend during all those venting sessions about Manuel. No man really wants to listen to a girl cry her heart out over some dude who has broken her heart, particularly if he knows that he would be a better guy for her. I remembered several occasions when I was upset about Manuel and Amir would try to cheer me up by bringing over popcorn and a movie. I had just broken up with Manuel, so Amir and I were only friends at the time; funny how quickly some things can change.

Amir looked at me with those mysterious eyes of his, and I tried my best not to crack a smile as he screwed up his face into a hilarious expression. I eventually surrendered and giggled, blinking away the few tears that dampen my eyelashes. I thanked him with a kiss for the foot massage. A few minutes and a few more kisses later, I got up from the sofa, put the dishes in the dishwasher and innocently called out to him from the kitchen. "Amir, are you ready for dessert yet?"

He appeared in the doorway of the kitchen within seconds, "Of course, but only if you can find a big enough platter," he said, grinning like the big bad wolf and walking towards me like a late-night snack.

Chapter 6

It's getting close to nine o'clock when we finish a game of strip chess, which was a new and decidedly more interesting version. I was also surprisingly dominant in the game; he seemed distracted, perhaps by what the rest of the evening might hold. Amir put away the board while I ran the fresh water in my whirlpool Jacuzzi that sits in the middle of my master bathroom. My bathroom is definitely my favorite feature in the apartment; the walls are candy-coated peach and it's a spacious oasis of soft towels, fragrant lotions, and an excess of luxurious toiletries. There are plants covering the windowsill and a stunning stained-glass door that separates it from the master bedroom.

I sprinkled the rose petals into the bubbling water and lit the peaches and cream candles that sent shadows dancing around the walls.

The mood was set and my favorite albums were on random, softly humming over the rumble of the Jacuzzi. I dropped my sarong to the floor and sank deep into the water. A moment later, Amir followed the trail of petals into the bathroom and stood at the entrance with a small platter of dipped strawberries and the chilled bottle of champagne.

He laid them down on a corner of the tub and pulled off his shirt. I felt a tingle of anticipation as I saw his chest muscles flex involuntarily. I reached over from inside the tub and unzipped his jeans. They fell to the floor and I took a good look at his naked form. I was enthralled by his flawless, muscled physique. I stretched out my hand, inviting him to join me.

He slid into the hot water, and I began playing a seductive game of licking my strawberry with my long narrow tongue. The heat of the room and my tongue's quick movements melted the chocolate; I could see Amir beginning to melt as well. I took a bite and a small stream of juice dripped down the sides of my mouth. He gently grabbed my jaw and licked once on each side, then laid a wet kiss on my lips. He also softly stroked the back of his knuckles down my cheek and looked into my eyes with a tender smile. He loved to touch my face and I didn't mind. As gorgeous as he is, he can touch anything he wants!

He popped the top of the bubbly and poured it into two gold-trimmed champagne glasses. I placed a small strawberry into his mouth and he bit down on half and motioned for me to take the other. Our lips pressed together once again and we rubbed noses, giggling at how comfortable and enamored we were with one another. Amir licked the sweet chocolate off my fingers and I was astonished by the way he sucked the tips so delicately. I started to feel some sparks and tingles between my legs that had nothing to do with the jets from the side of the tub.

Manuel never did this sort of stuff. He called romance soft, mushy shit. Well, I happened to love the occasional mushy romance, not that he ever cared.

"I think I owe you another foot rub," Amir said.

"Two massages in one day? You never even promised me one," I said with a playfully confused look on my face.

He gave me a sly grin and reminded me of last night. "Aren't your feet still sore from those stilettos?"

"You know what, they actually are," I replied as I stuck out my lips, like a pouting child hoping to get their way.

With all this attention on my feet, it's a good thing I got a pedicure today, I thought to myself.

The water was warm and set to the lowest cycle of bubbling. I lay back as Amir massaged one foot at a time. I closed my eyes and thought of us making love as his hands worked out the aches. I let out a soft, sensuous moan as he continued to knead my pressure points. He raised my foot from the water and kissed my toes softly. He slipped my big toe in his mouth and pressed his tongue on the bottom as he glided up and down. I pulled back, but he held on. It tickled and felt ridiculously good at the same time. He was immensely patient, and clearly didn't want to rush through the foreplay. I knew that he wanted me to be fully satisfied with his performance, which is a big plus.

He put my leg down, and I turned so my back rested against Amir's chest. We sat still and silently enjoyed a love song. I was definitely in the mood and from the bulge that had been growing against my back, so was Amir. He wrapped his arms around me, his hands lightly resting on my breasts and whispered in my ear. "Your skin is so soft; are you having a good time?"

"Of course, there's nowhere I'd rather be! Aren't you?" I said as I looked up at him, grinning dreamily.

"The only way I can describe it is a wet dream come true, Ayanna," Amir said as he squeezed me and laughed. I could feel his heart beating behind my head.

"You're so wonderful, Amir," I said as I reached around and felt his long locks. The tips were wet; so was I.

I love a man with dreads, and Amir clearly took good care of his. He used natural oils to moisturize them and keep them smelling good. I wanted to pull on them and force him inside of me, but I decided to behave like a lady and take it slow tonight. He started to sing along to the verses of a song from my favorite album. He's no Luther, but, he sings it so passionately that I don't mind the missed words. *"Baby, you're my consolation...I feel those sensations when I'm in your arms..."*

Chapter 7

He had lit the fireplace before coming into the tub, so after we dried off, we laid down a few thick blankets and pillows on the living room floor. It was unusually cold that night. Luckily, I didn't have to worry about being cold for long, because I had someone that I knew would keep me warm. The phone rang several times, but I let the answering machine pick up the messages. Chase knew better than to bother me tonight!

After it rang twice in a row, I reluctantly got up to answer it, in case it was urgent. "Johnston residence. Hello. Hello... who is this?" No answer. In the back of my mind, I had an idea of who it was, but instead of getting upset and wasting more of my precious time with Amir, I hung up the phone.

Amir looked confused when I returned, but I had no explanation for him. I simply sipped on my champagne and lounged beside him. I tried to keep my mind off the weird phone call, but I tensely waited for the phone to ring again. *Stop it, Zuria!* I should have focused on more important things...like the beautiful man lying next to me. I just didn't want him to get caught in the middle of anything...or get hurt.

I considered telling him that I had seen Manuel, but I didn't want him to think I was trying to make him jealous. I would have liked to warn him about the guy; Manuel had proven to be crazy and he'd fight over me in a heartbeat. That was the last thing I wanted to happen. I'm a grown ass woman and I don't need anyone fighting over me. That teenage fight-for-the-girl shit hadn't been attractive for a long time.

"Which scent do you like...spearmint or rosemary?" I asked.

"Any oil is fine," Amir said.

He had on a pair of red and black satin boxers and he turned over on his belly while I warmed the spearmint oil between my hands. I started at his shoulders taking my time and kneading down his smooth, hairless back. The scent is invigorating, yet soothing, and I feel his muscles relax beneath my hands.

He turned over smoothly and I rubbed his chest, being careful not to tug on the black, curly hairs. I followed a thin line of hairs to his boxers with my index finger, teasing him. He stared at me with intense emotion. I caught a glimpse of the crackling fire reflected in his eyes, fitting for the obvious signs of his burning love for me. I continued to massage his chest and kissed his hardened nipples.

He reached out for me and said, "I've been in love with you from the first moment I met you. I understand if you don't feel the same way yet, but I can only hope that you'll eventually see me as the one you've been searching for all these years. I'm never going to hurt you, Zuria, and I'll do whatever I can to protect you. I just want you to trust me."

"I feel the same way about you, Amir. You're like my knight in shining armor, but it's too soon and too damn surreal. I'm expecting myself to wake up at any moment."

"Trust me, it's real. Maybe I should show you just how real it is."

He stood up and went into his overnight bag.

I wondered what it could be as I watched him unzip his overnight bag. For a second, I had the crazy idea that it might be a ring. That would be a little too fast, even though I felt so strongly about him. We had barely scratched the surface of careers, ambitions, or our stance on having children. Who knows, maybe he doesn't want any children. My thoughts raced in those ten seconds of breathless anticipation. *Calm down, Zuria.* I silently lectured myself. *You haven't even seen what the damn thing is yet.*

I took several deep breaths as he handed me the gift. It was neatly wrapped in a small box with delicately subtle hearts on the sides. From the smile on my face, he knew I was nervous, but excited. I still saw that crackling fire in his eyes as he watched me open the box.

"It's a souvenir! I just couldn't wait until Valentine's Day," he said.

I looked inside, where a gold diamond locket with a chain sat nestled in a crumpled bed of satin. Inside the locket was a picture that we had taken on our first evening together in a "kissing booth". We had taken four pictures in a row and split the strip in half, two and two. I felt touched and relieved at the same time. A locket I could handle, a ring would be a bit much.

"Amir, it's beautiful. Wow...thank you."

"I'm willing to give you the world. Consider this a down payment."

"Amir, all I want is your heart. Everything else will fall into place."

His words were always so spontaneous, yet perfect. A poetic lover, indeed. At Sage's Jazz Cafe, I'd lay back in the cut literally dripping with passion for him. One night, on a recent freestyle Friday, he encouraged me to join him on stage. We were both surprised when I poured out my heart to him in rambling free verse.

He had no idea I felt that way about him until I stood there gazing into his eyes in a room full of people. It was one of the most terrifying and honest things I'd ever done in my life.

I was trembling visibly, Chase later told me, but I thought I did a decent job. I spoke from the soul, and it was obvious that it had been on my mind for a while. My memory is usually not great, but I doubt I'll forget what I said that night.

"My love for him is real and it keeps on getting stronger. His touch whispers secrets to my most secret spots. And, like empty bellies, they wail out in hunger. The taste of his lips is sweet. Divine. His smell is fresh like rain and summer wine. Damn, he's so fine! From this day forward I'll give one hundred percent; fifty isn't enough when my heart knows he's God sent."

He slid me down to the cozy pillows on the floor. He unhooked my red pajamas one button at a time. He stroked my breasts with the edible oil; they glistened with flickering fire under the shadows of his hands. He offered me a sip of bubbly and slowly poured the rest onto my already sizzling body. It sent a rush of cold through my body that faded as quickly as it appeared. Amir tasted my dark brown, erect nipples. Most women would kill to have nipples like mine. He traced slow circles around them and headed south.

Between the licking and the nibbling, every inch of me yearned for him. He guided his hands down the sides of my body as his tongue flicked into my belly button and lapped up some of the champagne that had gathered there.

"Oh, baby...you're too much," I moaned.

Amir looked at me for confirmation and showed those pearly white teeth. He moved lower, but first he kissed and sucked on my upper lip, leaving my knees weak and making me glad that I was already on the ground. He grabbed my bare bottom and slid a plush pillow under it, then stretched out in front of my open legs. His tongue quivered in an inexplicable movement and I reached for the ceiling and nearly clapped my hands. I caught myself and said, "Don't stop!" If he had, I might have held him with these thighs of mine. However, from the look in his eyes, Amir had no intentions of stopping.

I grabbed onto his dreads as I climaxed. He began to write his name with his tongue. A... m... and when he dotted the "i", I bit my lower lip as hard as I could. He took his precious time dotting the "i". My body began to tremble as if it was going into an epileptic seizure. I tried to stay sexy, but it's hard to do when you lose control of half your senses. I couldn't help but have a wild, primal gleam in my eye...it all felt too good. A...m...i......r!

"Turn over," Amir said calmly. He sounded like he meant business.

I love it when a man takes control, and oddly enough, when he's in control, the "beast" is more likely to come out. I did what I was told and turned over. I turned around and eyed him as he grabbed a condom and slid it on. Some women might be afraid of him because he's so well endowed. I happen to love those extra inches, especially because he knows how to use them.

He slapped and kissed my behind, sending goose bumps all over my body. He moved his warm body against mine as he gently dropped kisses all along my spine. He knew how to make the tension last, and make me want it even more. I felt his heartbeat against my back and I turned to kiss him. His lips are already pursed, waiting for me. He cradled my neck with his strong touch and our tongues tangled in my mouth.

Before we began, I took one final look at my poetic lover and said, "Amir, promise me one thing."

"Anything."

"If I die the way I want to, promise me you won't wipe the smile off my face!"

I ached for him and as he chuckled at my request, I gave him a proper "take me now" stare. He shook his head and smiled, so I closed my eyes and surrendered to his will. Apparently, we would take this time nice and slow.

Chapter 8

We lied in each other's arms, wrapped in a freshly washed comforter that seemed sewn with lavender. The previous night had been electrifying; I wished that I could live off love without having a drink or a bite to eat. I laughed to myself as I thought of Amir curling his toes uncontrollably when I rode him backwards. Lying next to me, Amir seemed like he was in deep thought.

How'd you sleep?" I asked.

"Like a bear in winter," Amir said as he wiped the dreams out of his eyes.

"Are you ready for breakfast?"

"Sure. We certainly worked up an appetite!" Amir said as he smiled and sat up, letting the sheets fall to his waist.

I told him to freshen up if he wanted while I made breakfast. I followed him out of the room, wearing only a tiny t-shirt, and he turned around outside of the hallway bathroom and said, "Damn. You're even more beautiful in the morning. I didn't think it was possible." He bit his lip, grunted and smacked me on my behind. He chased me down the hallway as I laughed uncontrollably at his smooth line. I grabbed my kitchen spatula and chased him back to the bathroom. I gave him a long kiss and returned to the kitchen, so pleased that the playful energy and passion hadn't faded at all overnight.

We discussed our plans for the next few weeks as we enjoyed our veggie omelets, buttered croissants and freshly squeezed orange juice. I was going to be swamped with work all week, so we wouldn't have any real time together until the following weekend. My job didn't stop when I left work, and it usually continued once I got home. However, I had made a promise to myself not to work too hard by giving myself the weekend off.

"Well, I actually have to go to Miami for a couple of weeks as well to get started on my next project. I'm really getting burnt out of the modeling business though. I'd love to get out of it in the next couple years and open my own chain of agencies," he said.

"Not a bad idea, Amir. When do you leave for Miami?"

"Tuesday morning. Flying, as usual!"

"Are you going to take those pills again?"

"Shiiit, of course! I don't think I've ever flown without them."

Amir doesn't care for flying. He told me that when he was a little boy, he'd hold onto his mother the whole time as they flew back and forth to London. He wouldn't even go to the airplane bathroom alone. That eternity of water always makes me want a double shot of cognac too, but I wasn't nearly as bad as Amir.

I wanted to catch up with my friends anyway, so the timing wasn't terrible for his trip to Miami. The good thing about Amir is that he liked hanging out with my friends, and he didn't mind if I went out with them alone. That was another major plus in my book! With Amir, it was easy to juggle my friendships and my relationship so no one felt left out. It was pretty damn close to perfect.

***

As I walked Amir to the door, he swept me off my feet with a wild embrace. He lost his balance and we both fell to the floor, laughing.

"I love you!" I said.

"I love you too!" he replied.

"Don't be checking out all those half-naked girls down there!"

"Well, I promise to imagine *your* face on them if I do."

Playfully, I punched him in the chest. I grabbed his shirt and pulled him close to me. "Is that supposed to make me feel special or something?"

"I'm only kidding!" he said.

Amir stood outside my door and put up his hands like he was saying a prayer. I was born at night, not last night. I know that all men take a peek sometimes, just like women. It's in our nature, and is perfectly fine with me, as long as you keep your hands to yourself.

"I know you are, sweetie!" I admitted.

"You be good too! Don't give away the good stuff, alright? Your man will be back Sunday after next."

"This is all for you, baby," I said, as I ran his hands down the sides of my body.

"Au revoir," he said.

"Bon voyage!" I countered, blowing him kisses. I stayed at my door, smiling, until Amir walked out of sight. The smile stayed on my face far longer.

Chapter 9

"What's up, poetry man?" Amir heard the voice from behind him and made a good guess about the source.

Amir was sitting at The Coffee Shop, getting his daily dose of caffeine and warming up with a White Chocolate Latte. He didn't respond to Manuel and acted as though he hadn't heard anything. He sat at his table by the window, reading a newspaper.

"How's my girl?" Manuel asked. He clearly wasn't going to give up, so Amir changed tactics. He turned slightly, still not looking at Manuel.

"She's being well taken care of," Amir replied, cold and emotionless.

"Were you there last night with her?"

Amir didn't like being baited, but now that he was in the situation, he realized that he also had no reason to lie. "I was. Was that you who called and forgot to speak?"

Manuel ignored the question, but responded with one of his own.

"Did she let you hit that pretty pussy?"

"Not your business. Why all the questions?"

"You know damn well why!" Manuel's voice was raised, and a few people in the otherwise quiet shop turned to stare.

"You should take a walk before things get ugly!" Amir wasn't one to back down, and he always followed through. He was a well-built guy, but so was Manuel.

Manuel said nothing, then called the server over and ordered a large coffee. He blatantly checked out the server's curvaceous figure and shook his head, smirking. Manuel looked back at Amir with enough hate and angry envy that Amir was taken aback for a moment.

"Did you forget about our conversation?" Manuel asked.

"I won't do it, man. Now go harass some other muthafucka!" Amir said. His blood was starting to boil.

"What'd you say to me? Man, we both know that I only have one call to make and your punk ass is history!"

Amir was visibly shaking now, and gripped the table with his free hand. He matched Manuel's savage gaze before speaking.

"Don't you care about her at all, man? Are you so selfish that you can't just let her be happy? She deserves to be with someone who'll give her what she wants and needs. That isn't you."

"Her place is with me!" Manuel barked.

"No it's not, and neither is her heart!" Amir shouted as he pounded the table.

"What, so you think she loves some uppity pretty boy like you? Get tha fuck outta here!"

"Get over it, Manuel! I care about her enough to tell her how I feel. That's more than your pimped out pussy ass could ever do!"

Manuel is clearly enraged; the blood has rushed to his face.

"If you touch Zuria again, you'll be sorry, muthafucka!" Manuel said as he clenched his fists.

Most of the other customers in the cafe have noticed the confrontation and are watching the commotion between the two infuriated men. The mood in the café has become uncomfortable, and some of them had already quickly finished their coffees and were preparing to leave. The manager of the café was heading towards them, clearly planning to escort Manuel and Amir outside. Manuel gives him a disdainful look and curses at him, as though daring the manager to lay his hands on him. A security guard that neither of them had noticed approached Manuel from behind and restrained him as he shoved him forcefully outside. The main areas in Atlanta had a nearly constant police presence, and a squad car from half a block away pulled up in front of the café when the commotion rolled out into the street.

"I feel sorry for your mama, Puta!" Manuel said as an officer pushed Manuel's head down and shoved him into the back of the car. Manuel was no stranger to the police, and it didn't take much of an explanation from the security guard for the officers to make the decision over who had instigated the fight.

Not one to take an insult lightly, Amir's first reaction was to grab Manuel's throat through the police car window. However, he thought of Zuria, and the man that he wanted to be for her, so he quickly pressed his middle finger against the window, smiled and walked away.

Chapter 10

I had been missing Amir's touch, smile and sense of humor for almost a week; I couldn't get him off my mind. I hadn't been sleeping, and my appetite had practically disappeared. I didn't know if that was a sign of love or that I was just somewhat crazy, quite lonely, and really horny.

I'd been going to the gym with Chase about three times a week for almost a year now, and I knew everyone's business that went to the gym on a regular basis. Women love to talk in locker rooms, and Chase was oddly good at dragging gossip out of men as well. Frankly, most of them are married and single guys who can't seem to focus on the main reason why they're at the gym in the first place. I had gotten used to being an object of their attention, and I was good at ignoring their stares and less than subtle gestures. I just imagined them as lonely puppy dogs drooling over a delicious treat.

If I could read their minds when I walk by in my spandex pants and sports bra, I'd probably be disgusted. I had been talking to Chase about buying some equipment for my place, since that kind of attention had gotten pretty annoying week after week. Of course, he disagreed with me. He always had a silly perspective on things like that.

"Girl, are you serious? This place is a goldmine! It's like a buffet in here with all these sweaty hunks working their sexy bodies into shape. Damn! The meat is Grade-A select in this joint."

"Don't you ever stop?"

"Hell no...not while I'm breathing!"

Chase grabbed his throat and started to make gasping sounds.

"Don't go tempting God now. Baby, it's been almost three hours. You ready to go?"

"Yeah...I guess I have worked up an appetite!" Chase said as he watched a young Japanese guy do bench presses a few feet away.

"Well, at least you don't discriminate, do you?" I asked rhetorically.

"I don't when he looks like that Bing Li dude," he said as he laughed and kicked his legs in the air.

"If his last name is spelled L-I, then you've got the right one. He's the sexy Japanese guy."

"They all look the same to me, girlfriend - slim and oh so fine."

"Alright, I guess I'll give you that!"

Chase and I left the gym, laughing and elbowing one another with jokes about our foreign fantasies.

***

It was Thursday, which meant only one thing – four more days until Amir returned from Miami. I had a few students waiting to talk to me about their personal problems, but I could barely focus. Sunday night with my man was the only thing I could think about. It had been a crazy week for me and I'd been working nonstop. Luckily, that meant Amir was only on my mind for about 10 hours a day, rather than 24.

I had been counseling Elise Jefferies, a female student who recently had a baby. She was seriously considering quitting school because she didn't have anyone to care for her daughter while she went to school all day.

"Elise, who's been watching the baby while you're here at school?" I asked her during our appointment.

It was late Thursday afternoon in my office.

"Her father does. He's older than I am; he already graduated."

"Does he work?"

"Yeah. He works nights. He said that he won't be able to watch the baby anymore though, because he found a first shift job that pays a lot more."

I felt so sorry for that child, and I didn't just mean the baby. She was only sixteen and didn't know how to raise herself, let alone a newborn! Although I was concerned for the student, my mind began to wander, thinking about Amir. Was he missing me like I was missing him? I collected myself and continued to ask the necessary questions.

"So, are you going to continue living with your parents?"

"I don't know. They told me to stay in school, but my boyfriend wants me to move in and watch the baby at home."

"Elise, I have all the resources you need so you can stay in school and still take care of your baby. It's an alternative school for young mothers. These days, there are a lot of opportunities for young teenage mothers who want to finish their education. You have options. Of course you want to provide for your child, but for the sake of your own future, you've got to stay in school. Don't give up on yourself. Alright, Elise?"

"Yes, ma'am."

"Sweetie, my mother's a ma'am. You can call me Miss Johnston."

"Yes, Miss Johnston!"

"Why don't you come back after your lunch break and I'll give you some more information about this alternative program. Keep your head up! You're a smart girl, and with some support you're going to be just fine," I said as she headed for the door. I saw her smile as she shook her head in agreement.

Every time those children left my office, I would say a little prayer. I knew that some of them wouldn't take my advice, but I also knew that some would. As much as I hated to admit it, it was a numbers game. I was always proud of myself for at least trying to help all of them. A lot of the days were hard, and depressing, but I couldn't let my emotions get the best of me. I had to be strong for them.

I had another student who was allegedly being abused by his father, so I had to fit him into my schedule. Why did these people keep having children if they didn't have the patience for it? It was no wonder that there were so many runaways in this country. I would get tired of being slapped across the face too. I couldn't even count the number of malnutrition cases I've seen. Half of those parents had perfectly fine jobs, but they cared more about entertaining their drunken friends every weekend than putting food on the table. After years of doing this job, when a child came into the safety of my office, the stories they would tell weren't even unbelievable anymore, just heartbreaking.

Chapter 11

Friday finally arrived, and Amir would be back on Sunday. I called my job and took a sick day, because I couldn't seem to get any sleep last night. I had terrible heartburn after I ate dinner, so I stayed on the sofa and played with Scribbles. By noon, I felt much better, and three hours later, I went to an African salon to get my hair braided. I did my weekly shopping and filled my 2007 BMW with Super Premium gasoline. Manuel and I had decided to get matching BMWs; his was blue, mine was candy apple red. If I didn't love that car so much, I would have gotten rid of it just to distance myself from those memories, but that car was too beautiful to give up.

I heard Chase's voice speaking into my answering machine as I unlocked my door, but I couldn't get to the phone in time to pick up. There were two other messages, so I set my groceries on the kitchen floor and pressed play.

"Hello, Zureelya Johnson. It's Bob from…"

"Delete! Come on Bob, get the name right before you call!" I said to myself as I walked back to the kitchen. Bob, whatever he wanted, would not be getting a returned call.

I listened to the next message.

"Hey, Zuria. I didn't want to call you while you were out driving, but I thought you should know as soon as possible…"

Chase paused. He sounded like he was talking to someone nearby. "Sweetie, Manuel was in a terrible accident this morning;

he's in bad shape. I knew that you would want to know right away. Please call me when you get this. I love you."

I had been putting away the eggs as the message had begun; I barely realized that I had dropped them until they splattered onto my shoes. Everything around me went fuzzy, like some slow motion dream scene. My head began to spin and I grabbed for the edge of the counter to support myself. I reached for the paper towels and wiped off my shoes and picked up the carton that was oozing the remains of a dozen eggs. My mind was racing and the tears began to fall before I even realized. Shaking the shock from my head, I immediately picked up the phone to call Chase. The answering machine picked up, so I called his cell phone. The space between rings sounded like an eternity. It rang four times, but it may as well have been 400. He could immediately hear that I was crying, nearly hysterical.

"Zuria? Hey. Honey, take a deep breath. Talk to me."

My nose was leaking like a faucet and I could feel the tears streaming off my face onto my chest.

"Is he...?" I began, unable to finish the question.

"No, baby, but he's in the ICU. Listen to me...I want you to sit down okay. Chill out, there's nothing you can do right now. I'm on my way, alright?"

I hung up the phone and sank to the floor against the fridge; I didn't care that I had sat directly in the puddle of eggs on the floor. I stared blankly at the cabinets in front of me, trying to slow my breathing and will myself to stop weeping until I heard his truck pull up. I ran outside and nearly knocked over my neighbor, Mr. Baker.

Mr. Baker is an old, Jewish man who had been living here long before me. He was a nice enough man, but he had become lonely and bitter after his wife died a year ago. Like plenty of old white people, large groups of black folks seemed to set him on edge. When Chase and his happy-go-lucky friends came over, you'd best believe that Mr. Baker was watching.

I stopped at the exit to catch my breath. I hunched over and held onto my knees as my heart raced; my head was still spinning and my chest hurt from the pounding of my heart. Chase walked me to his truck, leaned me gently against it and began to explain.

"Baby, Manuel was drunk driving and speeding like a madman. He swerved to avoid a kid in the street and ran right into a fire hydrant. He wasn't wearing a seatbelt; he went through the windshield. If you want to go over there, I'll take you to the hospital."

Chase hadn't cared for Manuel since day one. However, he cared a hell of a lot about me, and my heart. He knew that Manuel was bad news, but he knew that I had loved him. I would never wish for anything like this to happen to Manuel, or anyone for that matter. I got in his truck without saying a word and he followed my lead and swung back out of the driveway.

***

We arrived at Atlanta General Hospital and I silently took a seat while Chase asked for Manuel Torres at the desk. I was trembling so hard that the woman beside me laid her hand on my shoulder to reassure me, saying something about the power of prayer. I overheard the nurse say that Manuel was out of surgery and was recovering in a private suite. She gave Chase the room number and he led me by the arm as we looked for Room 804.

Chase opened the door as quietly as he could; Manuel was sound asleep, probably from the anesthesia or the pain meds. He wasn't moving at all and I couldn't even see his chest rise and fall. He was just lying there, calm and peaceful, as though he hadn't just flown through a windshield. I walked along the side of his bed to hold his hand. Not only was he unresponsive, but he was also cold and rigid. Chase stood beside me and rubbed my back in silent support.

For some reason, I felt slightly guilty for being there.

I had told Manuel that I didn't love him anymore, yet there I stood by his side in this cold, sterile hospital room. Even more than that, I also felt guilty for being there while Amir was away and had no idea what was going on. How would I feel if Amir sobbed and held the hand of an injured ex while I was away on business? I certainly wouldn't like it, but I would hopefully be supportive of him, as I hoped he would be when I told him about all this madness that happened while he was in Miami.

The nurse came in to check his blood pressure, nodded her head at both of us, and left the room. Manuel's doctor stood at the doorway as he talked and laughed with another doctor in the hallway. A little consideration would have been nice, although he hadn't noticed that there were visitors in the room yet.

He looked surprised to see us and quickly changed his demeanor from the hallway. "Good afternoon, I'm Dr. Gordon. And you are...family or friends?"

Chase was annoyed by his tone, so he took a seat in the corner and said nothing, leaving it up to me.

"Friends," I answered. It felt very strange calling the man I use to love a friend; I had never had to answer a question like that before.

Dr. Gordon got straight to the point. "Mr. Torres has suffered a spinal injury. His jaw and left arm are also broken. His jaw had to be wired shut, so he won't be able to speak for 4-6 weeks. However, the difficult news is that it is unclear how serious the spinal injury is; there is a chance of paralysis. In the coming days, we'll know more, and we hope that with extensive therapy and support, there could be a chance that he will walk again."

I felt my head start to swim and my vision blurred, like it had in my kitchen, but far worse this time. It felt like my head had been crashed between two cymbals, like in those silly cartoons. That was the last thought I had before I collapsed at Dr. Gordon's feet. It happened so fast that he didn't even have time to catch me. I heard my head hit the ground, but didn't have time to feel it before everything went black.

***

"Miss Johnston, are you alright?" a night nurse was leaning over me, checking my blood pressure, and clearly waiting for an answer.

"Where am I?"

"You're in the hospital. You fainted while visiting your friend Mr. Torres," she explained.

Chase came into the room looking distraught, drinking a bottle of water. When he saw that I was awake, his face brightened considerably.

"Zuria, you scared the shit out of me! How are you?"

"I'm really cold. Is Manuel awake yet?"

He didn't answer. Instead, he covered me with a thin blanket that had been lying at the foot of my bed. I started to pull myself into a sitting position, and looked around for my purse and my pants. Somehow, they had gotten me out of my clothes and into one of those damn hospital gowns. Seeing that I was getting agitated, the nurse gently, yet firmly, insisted that I stay put and rest for a while. Turning to Chase, I assumed he would back me up and be the voice of reason.

"Chase, I need to get out of here; I can't stand hospitals. You know that I watched my sister die in one. Let's go."

"Chill, baby girl. The nurse is right," Chase said.

"Chase, what's the matter?"

He hadn't completely wiped that concerned, baffled look off his face yet, and once again, he didn't answer me. I didn't bother to ask again. I just did what I was told and dropped my head back onto the soft, propped up pillows.

"Be patient, dear. You should be able to leave within the hour," the nurse said.

"Thanks," I replied, though my tone was far from grateful.

A doctor entered the room the moment the nurse left. I immediately noticed her energy and effortless grace. She shook my hand as if she was running for Congress, and she was someone I'd probably vote for. "Miss Johnston, I'm Dr. Levitz. How are you feeling?"

"Pretty strange. What's going on?"

"Well, we ran a few tests and it looks like your iron is abnormally low. Do you take any vitamins or dietary supplements?"

"Sometimes...I mean, when I remember to take them."

She paused and looked at Chase. He was staring right at me from across the room, but he looked fidgety. He crossed and uncrossed his legs and patted his knees to some silent rhythm. Chase wasn't a nervous person; this situation was getting strange, and I was losing patience.

"Alright, could someone just tell me what the hell is going on here?"

"Miss Johnston, are you aware that you're pregnant?" Dr. Levitz asked.

"Come again?" I said, genuinely thinking that I'd misheard her.

"Miss Johnston, you're pregnant," she said.

For the third time in three hours, my head felt as though it had been struck by lightning. The combined weight of the day was too much, and the tears began to pour, cascading down my cheeks. I could feel the panic settling in; that clawing, grasping feeling in my stomach and my throat began to climb. My body began to shake as I looked up to the ceiling, to where God was supposed to be. *Could it get any worse?*

Chase quickly stepped in and told the doctor about my panic attacks, then took one of my hands and squeezed it tight.

The cool and collected doctor instructed me to breathe, as though I had forgotten.

"Zuria? You have to calm down; just count slowly to ten. And breathe," she said, but I was more focused on Chase's presence beside me as I gulped for air and prayed it would stop the rising tide of fear in my chest.

"You're gonna be fine, sweetie," Chase said as he laid his arm across my back and kissed me on the top of my head.

I smelled his classic aftershave scent coming lightly from his face. It calmed me and I closed my eyes. Sometime later, I felt Chase lay my head back on the pillow, but I was already fading into sleep.

***

Disoriented, I woke up and had a short moment of panic before looking around the room. Chase was sitting in a chair next to me, talking on the phone. He smiled at me, held up one finger, and said goodbye to the person on the other line.

"Where's Dr. Levitz?" I asked.

"She had to go check on another patient. I'll go see if she's around, okay?" he said.

"Thanks, Chase."

Dr. Levitz came in a few moments later and affectionately patted my leg, just above the knee. She came across as a very nurturing woman, and reminded me of my mother in a strange way. Something about the way she walked and how she felt comfortable touching people after knowing them for a very short time. I wished that my mother had been in the room with me.

"So...how far along am I?"

"I would say...about three months," Dr. Levitz said.

"Thr...three months?" I swallowed hard, hoping that I would wake up in my bed at home, and remember this conversation as nothing more than a bad dream. "Please, tell me you're kidding!" I blurted out; the surging panic began to rumble in my stomach again.

My world was crumbling right before my eyes. It didn't take a calendar or a PhD to know that it was Manuel's baby. Amir and I never had sex without protection, and besides, this had to have happened before Amir and I even slept together that first night. Chase saw what the news was doing to me, and stood by my side.

"Chase, what am I supposed to do now? I can't tell Amir about this baby! It would break his heart; I'd lose him. But I can't have an abortion! Dammit!" I cried out, sobbing into Chase's chest as he sat on the edge of my bed.

"Miss Johnston, I suggest you make an appointment with your Ob-Gyn for a full examination. Depending on your decision, you also need to start on your prenatal vitamins right away. Good luck, Zuria," Dr. Levitz said. With a final reassuring pat on my leg, she left the room.

Before we left, I finished filling out the paperwork in a daze; Chase grabbed my purse and we walked out of the hospital in silence.

We went back to my place. Chase insisted that he stay the night with me, which wasn't a bad idea, considering that I hadn't stopped crying since we had left the hospital. Chase had stayed over in the past, on those nights when I needed someone to be there. He'd make me food, hold me when I started to cry, or just lay a blanket over me that I'd find in the morning. He's always cared about me so much. Having a friend like Chase made me feel secure, special, and loved. I knew that this would be the kind of night where I would need some comfort. Everything seemed broken, and there was no one in the world I needed more than my best friend.

Chapter 12

The next day, I visited Manuel in the hospital. I was so exhausted from the night before that I could barely think straight, but I felt like being there was the right choice. Manuel awoke and looked at me, his surprised eyes were his only way to communicate with his jaw wired shut. It was the first time I had ever been able to talk to him without being interrupted, smacked or cursed out for something. I still didn't know if being there was a good idea, but I sat on his bed, took out a small blue book, and began to read him a story.

"This book is about a girl who fell in love with a guy. This guy carelessly macked on all the honeys, drank as much as he wanted and hung out with his crew...sometimes all night, leaving his girlfriend home alone. One day, she had enough and decided to end the relationship, but he refused to let her go. He went into a rage and slapped her across the face, busting her lip. He also threatened to slit her throat if she ever tried to leave him again. She told him that she'd had enough of the emotional, mental and physical abuse. She left him for good and didn't worry about his threats. She soon found a prince and he took her to a land where there was nothing but love, compassion, and trust. They were married and lived happily ever after."

I could see a tear rolling sideways down Manuel's cheek. Maybe he was sad because he couldn't get up and knock my ass on the floor. Or maybe because he was literally speechless; he couldn't curse me out with his jaw wired shut. However, I could imagine all the nasty things he'd like to say at the moment, I had definitely heard most of them before.

I took a step closer to him and said, "Manuel, this is my personal journal. That was my life when I was with you, summed up in a single page. It's a sad story, don't you think? No one in their right mind would stay in a relationship like the one that we had. Maybe that was the problem. Somehow I had lost my mind when I was with you. Luckily, I found it again."

I turned away and looked down at my hands. I had still been wearing the promise ring he gave me when we first started dating. I stared at my fingers as I tried to gather the right words in my mind. He deserved to know why I came that day, and I deserved to finally say it.

"I love Amir. He's my source of wisdom, energy, happiness...hope. He doesn't make me sad, or hit me, or take advantage of how much I care about him. I love him very much. I may even marry him some day."

Manuel was very silent, and he could only speak with his eyes, but they said enough. They were dark and lonely. I took my journal and began to tear it up in front of him, one page at a time. I balled up each page and threw them in the trash bin beside his bed. Some pieces landed in the bin and others didn't.

Afterwards, I gathered myself and looked directly into his haunted eyes. "That was my past, and now I'm looking forward to my future. Manuel, I have to let you go for good. This is where we part ways for good."

I took off his ring and laid it on the dresser. I lightly kissed his forehead and wished him luck with everything. His injuries would take a long time to heal; his future was uncertain, but my absence in it was not. I grabbed my handbag and headed for the door at the same time as his family was coming in. We exchanged a few, polite words in passing before I left without looking back.

**

Amir would be back the following day, so I still had a bit more time to decide how to tell him I was pregnant. If he didn't want to be with me anymore, I would understand. Raising a baby alone would be hard, but I wasn't going back to Manuel, that's for damn sure. I had the savings and the patience to do it, but it would certainly change every aspect of my life. *I guess that is what babies do to people, isn't it?* I thought to myself. I was starting to understand how all of my teen mothers felt when they sat down in my office for the first time. I still didn't understand how the hell I didn't know that I was pregnant? I had monthly periods, but they were usually light, and I would never have called myself "regular". Frankly, I thought I was beginning to go through "the change". Even though I was a bit young, it wasn't unheard of. I wasn't all that unhappy; periods were something I could definitely live without.

I soaked myself in a ginger bath. *I hope this doesn't hurt the baby...Oh god, listen to me talking about 'the baby' already...* I thought. I couldn't stop thinking about Amir. What would his response be when I told him that I was having a baby that was put in me by some other man? It's not like I cheated on him or anything, but the timing was terrible. I must have conceived right before we started dating. *Dammit, Manuel!*

Before we started dating, I would occasionally chat with Amir at the Jazz Lounge, but it was simply platonic. *Enough, Zuria!* I berated myself; I just needed thirty minutes of peace. I covered my face with a hot washcloth and sank as deep as I could into the sudsy, warm water.

After climbing out of the soothing bath, I massaged my body with lotion. I paused halfway through to feel my belly. I hadn't recognized the bulge until that moment; I really needed to pay more attention. I felt a little fluttering sensation, but I assumed that it was just my angry stomach still recovering from all the cheese pizza that I had been eating. My diet was basically a joke at that point. I stood in the middle of the room naked, rubbing my growing belly.

After a bit of self-reflection, I gathered my pink robe around my shoulders and put on my slippers. I realized that I haven't eaten all morning, so I fixed a big bowl of bran cereal. When I'm alone and want to escape from life for a while, I love to eat cereal and curl up watching "Knifetime" movies. I turned one on, but found it too depressing, even for that notoriously tragic channel. I decided to give my parents a call instead. I knew that they were on vacation in St. Croix and I didn't want to ruin it, but sometimes the only thing that will make you feel better is your mama on the other side of a telephone.

"Mama?"

"Well, hello there baby girl!"

I love it when she calls me baby girl. It reminded me of being so young and innocent. Unfortunately, I had called to let her know that her baby girl was all grown up and was having a baby of her own...I was not so young and innocent anymore.

"Ma... how are you and dad doing?"

"We're taking it one day at a time, honey. Today, we're going to the African Dance Festival to shake our hips out of place."

We both laughed hard, but my laughter turned into tears.

"What's the matter, Zuria?"

I could hear my father talking in the background.

"Well, obviously there is a lot to it, but I should probably just cut to the headline...I'm pregnant and Manuel is the father."

There was a brief pause. I hadn't planned out how I was going to break the news, but that wouldn't have been it. I probably should have given a bit of backstory, particularly about my love for Amir, Manuel's accident, or a dozen other shifting parts.

But, my mother had always been a sensible woman, and had my back as always.

"Darling, I know that you're a strong woman and that you know how to take care of yourself. You've always been a thinker; I know you'll make the right decision." She was always so sure of herself, and also trusted me so much. I wanted her to have a bit more of the story, however, because my father would surely have plenty of questions once she got off the phone.

"I'm not calling to tell you that I'm getting back with Manuel. I really love Amir. As in...I want to be with him for the rest of my life. But this baby...I haven't told either of them about it, Chase is the only one who knows. I mean, I'm not sure I even want to tell Manuel; he's going through enough already. He was in a car crash last week, a really bad one."

"Oh God! Baby girl, I think you've got to tell both of them, just not right now. First, get your thoughts together. You have to take care of yourself first, baby girl, not to mention the little one inside you. I did have a dream about a fish last month, but I didn't want to scare you. I know you don't put much stock in my dream analysis," my mother chuckled.

I laughed along with her; I felt so much better about everything with my mom on the line.

"Zuria, I can get on the next plane back to Atlanta if you want me to."

"I'd love to see you, but I'll be fine. Honestly. I'll call you guys next week with an update. Tell dad I said hello!"

"Okay. Be safe, Z. I love you!"

"Love you too. Bye, Ma!"

I was relieved, and somewhat surprised, that I hadn't gotten chewed out. I was just lucky that my mom answered the phone. I'd much rather have her explain everything to my father instead of me.

Chapter 13

Later that night, I called Chase to thank him again for being there for me the past few days, and to tell him what I had done at the hospital with my journal about Manuel. I told him that I had to let go and let God. Why is it that when we find ourselves in trouble, we also start finding some religion? Chase agreed that I had made the right choice.

Seeing Chase next to me in the hospital when I woke up had reminded me of how much we had been through together. A few years ago, he was brutally beaten by a bunch of homophobes while attending a pride parade. It's crazy to me how ignorant some people can be; they don't understand that being gay doesn't mean you're some sadistic, sexual predator. In fact, Chase is one of the most amazing human beings I've ever known!

When he was injured, I nursed him back to health; his family never came around much. We've always been there for each other, through thick and thin, and I've always supported the fact that he was a gay man. I've had to defend Chase and myself multiple times when people decided to say something about it, even when those people were his relatives. I couldn't help it; I had to put people in their places when they started talking that crazy shit to me. They always told me to stop hanging out with homosexual men before I turned gay myself! In those moments, I'd like to turn around like Sophia in that one movie and give them a solid smack. However, I tried to be the bigger person, so instead of fighting, I'd just tell them to mind their own damn business. Most of the time, it came from older people stuck in their outdated ways, but not always.

"Honey, you really are crazy! You didn't get escorted out of there, did ya?" Chase said, laughing hysterically.

"Actually, I was surprisingly calm the whole time. I didn't want to be too much of a bitch; he's in pretty rough shape."

"Did you mention the baby?"

"No. I'm not sure I want to tell him about it. He'll eventually find out anyway. I just don't want the hassle right now. He probably doesn't either."

"Well, how are you feeling, sweetheart? Do you need me to bring you anything?" As always, Chase was willing to be anything I needed, whether that was a nurse, confidant, drinking buddy, or gossiping girlfriend.

"No, babe, that's alright. Thanks, though. I think I just want to be alone for a while. Are you still going out tonight?" I asked.

"No. I'd rather come over and chill with my girl. You know that I'll make your favorite meal...Veggie Minestrone, garlic bread, side salad..." he trailed off, tempting me and my appetite.

"Mmm...that does sound good. Listen, I'm going to lay down for a bit. If I feel better when I wake up, I'll call you, okay?"

"I'll take it. I'm just on the other side of the phone. If you need me for anything, I'm here."

"Thanks, Chase. You're the best."

"Yeah, yeah, yeah...I love you too."

I lay down on my leather sofa and my thoughts wandered to my childhood years, back when everything was carefree, painless, and innocent. I jumped up and went to my bedroom closet, suddenly overcome by a desire to see my memory box, a dusty container with loads of my personal treasures from my past. I sat on my bedroom floor and shuffled through the pictures of my childhood sweethearts. Most of them had only been silly crushes, but at the time, they were everything to me! There was Malcolm, with the high top fade, Quincy, the wannabe R&B singer, and of course,

Darnell, the breakdancer. I used to daydream about them all day during class, during dinner, while I was doing homework, and a thousand other moments of the day.

I never built up the courage to talk to them about my crush. My parents had taught me to be a lady. My dad believed that men should open the doors, push in the women's chairs, and be the one to ask ladies on the dates. Since his dating days, I suppose a lot had changed. Women have become independent, which is something to be proud of, but it doesn't mean that they should judge every man by some impossible standard or expect constant equality. There's nothing wrong with a man showing a bit of chivalry. I know that I do my share as a woman.

After the nostalgia of those pictures, I took my favorite baby doll from the box. I had plenty of dolls back in the day, but nothing close to this one. It looks almost perfectly preserved, with brown Shirley Temple curls and big eyelashes. Also, it's dressed in brand new clothes that my mother sewed for her. When my mother gave me this doll, she told me to never be afraid of anything, except for God. I can admit it now; I was practically afraid of my own shadow for most of my childhood. I slept with this doll so it would protect me from the scary people yelling and marching outside our house at night.

Twenty-five years later, I was sitting in my own room, in my very own apartment, yet the doll still made me feel safe. I daydreamed back to when my sister and I would play dress up for hours. Nadia was my best friend. Even though she was younger by two years, she would stick up for me when the school girls would circle me and pull on my long, thick hair.

My mother is Christian, but when she married my father, she learned a lot about his cultural traditions. She put Bantu braids in our hair and dressed us in homemade, tribal-looking clothes. For some reason, many of the other children hated us for being different. I quickly learned to toughen up and taught them about our lifestyle. Eventually, they left us alone, and some even befriended us. So often, people are scared of change, and things that are different. It only takes some effort and patience to set things straight.

When I entered college, I changed everything about myself.

I felt as though I was taking control over my own life for the first time. Many of the morals and values were still embedded within me, but I had to go out and find Zuria...the person that *I* wanted to be.

During my years in college, I became curious about the boys outside of my race. I had been pretty sheltered as a child, so I even wondered if they ate the same foods and watched the same movies. The strangest thing I ever did was keep my eye out for any outline in their pants to see if they were as big as the black men that I knew. Perhaps it was comfort, or the influence of my family, but for whatever reason, I always found myself drawn back to my own race.

***

I woke up with a stretch and a yawn, only to find myself in the dark. I turned on the touch lamp; the clock above the fireplace said 7:57 p.m. I was starving, and the sounds coming from my stomach agreed. The rumbling in my belly was probably what woke me up. I drank a glass of cold water to shock my system awake, then remembered that Chase was expecting my call. I grabbed my cordless phone to call him, but the answering machine picked up. That boy was never at home. I figured that he had decided to go out after all, so I called his cell phone.

I should have called the cell phone first, it seems to be connected to his hip 24/7. It rang twice before he picked up.

"Hey, sleepy head!"

"Hey, babe! I'm sorry for not calling earlier; I fell asleep hard...my body needed it, I guess. Forgive me?"

"Don't worry about it, sugar. Just get back in bed and I'll see you tomorrow."

"Okay. Are you at Koko's?"

"Zuria, you know Koko's ain't the same without you. Besides, I'm over at a friend's house."

The tone of his voice sounded soft and elegant, and he hadn't cussed once. I knew him well enough to know that something was up; Chase was probably interested in more than "friendship" with that mystery companion.

"Guy or girl?"

"You're so crazy, Z!" he yelled and laughed right into my ear.

"He must be next to you, right?"

"Uh huh."

"Alright, Chase...have fun. Don't do anything I wouldn't do!"

"In that case, I've got plenty to do, honey!" Chase said teasingly. We hung up.

I made myself a turkey and cheese sandwich with some tortilla chips and a dill pickle on the side. With a tall glass of milk in hand, I headed for my bedroom. I climbed up on my high king-size canopy bed and turned on the tube. Nothing interesting was on, per usual, just a bunch of commercials of people selling useless products. I was taking the last bite of my sandwich when I heard the phone ring. The caller ID read "unknown call". That didn't narrow it down much; it could be anyone calling from my family and friends. On the other hand, it could be another telemarketer, despite my request to be put on the 'Do Not Call' list.

The phone continued to steadily ring, so I decided to pick up before the machine did.

"Johnston residence."

I heard a deep, mellow voice laid over loud music in the background.

"Hello, Zuria. It's your favorite Miami model." Amir said.

I froze. My hand went numb holding the phone.

"Zuria?" he said. I took a deep breath before answering.

"Hey, Amir! Sorry, I couldn't hear you that well; I just heard music and voices in the background. How are you?"

"Sorry about that, babe. I'm at the Caribbean Café with a few co-workers. I just wanted to call and tell you that I miss you. I hope everything is going well. Excited to hear from me?"

I hesitated to inform him about my unbelievable weekend, he sounded like he was in such a good mood. Instead, I put on my happy face, despite him not being able to see me, and took another long, deep breath.

"I miss you, too, and of course I'm excited! Are you still coming back tomorrow?"

"Yeah, I'm leaving as soon as possible. I'm ready to go! I haven't seen so many fake, plastic-looking people in my whole life. Everyone looks like wannabe models and they walk around looking like they're on a red carpet 24/7," Amir chuckled.

"I bet those people never leave home without makeup and designer sunglasses, huh?"

"You know it! These two weeks have been dragging! I've been working twelve or fourteen hours a day. I barely had time for dreams, besides one or two of you. I can't wait to put my arms around you, baby."

He must have been tipsy; he only calls me baby when he's a few pints in. He has called me 'beautiful' and 'bubble butt', but not baby. I didn't mind, it sounded sexy.

"I can't wait to hold you, too. Is there anything interesting going on tonight?"

"Well, the guys and I are getting ready to play a few games of pool. Basically, I'm about to kick ass and take some names!"

I heard the guys in the background disagreeing with his bold claim, shouting and letting their testosterone speak for itself. Once Amir's co-workers got away from their wives and girlfriends, it was like they were in college again! That being said, they were all nice, respectful guys most of the time.

I wrapped myself deeper into my comforter.

I heard a male voice in the background, "Hey, Zuria! Will you marry me?"

"Who was that?" I asked, smiling at his silly friends.

"Damian," Amir said, his tone slightly annoyed.

"Oh, that white guy from France?"

"Yep. That's the one."

I heard smooching sounds in the background, most likely aimed at Amir, or more accurately, me.

"Assez-vous, s'il vous plait! Don't get fucked up!" Amir shouted away from the phone.

I sensed a little bit of jealousy, which was flattering. Then I heard some commotion that sounded like people were fighting.

"What's going on?" I asked.

"The usual. These guys are just dickheads when they have a few drinks. Anyways, it was really good to hear your voice. I'll call you when I arrive tomorrow, okay?" Amir asked.

"Alright. Good night, Amir!"

"Night, babe."

I lay awake staring at the ceiling as the full moon shined in through my bedroom window. It was pretty quiet in the neighborhood, no heavy traffic or loud house parties. That was a good thing. The following day I had a full day ahead of me, which meant a serious need for beauty sleep. I still hadn't found the words to tell Amir about both my good and bad news. I hoped that my heart would know what to say when the moment was right.

I watched Scribbles climb into her bed, following my lead. I held my pillow tight and looked over at the empty space where Amir's head had been, and where I hoped it would be again soon. The scent of him was gone; I had washed my sheets the day after he slept over. I closed my eyes, took a series of slow, deep breaths and prayed, using feelings more than actual words. I was asleep before I realized it, yet my dreams filled with strange possibilities, both good and bad, for my future.

Chapter 14

I had been waiting all day for Amir to come home, but he hadn't called all through Sunday morning. I considered that he might want to unpack and unwind before coming to see me, which was understandable. By early afternoon, I had run out of things to do. My clothes were ironed and lunch was packed and ready for Monday. I had also written myself a note to call my doctor for an exam first thing tomorrow morning. I tried to stay optimistic and prayed that Amir wouldn't leave me after he found out that I was pregnant.

In my musing on what Amir might do, I thought of how conniving men can be, just as much as women. I knew what Manuel thought; if he kept me barefoot and pregnant, my resolve would weaken. I would fall completely into submission, and never have the confidence to leave him. I suppose part of the blame rested on me for allowing him to control me as much as he did. Mainly, I shouldn't have let him talk me out of staying on birth control. I spent four and a half years waiting for him to propose to me. Then, when the relationship was at its worst, and my freedom from him was about to begin, I ended up getting pregnant. Anyways, there was no reason to cry about it, I promised myself not to shed another tear. What's done was done!

After my third trip to the bathroom in what seemed like only an hour, I heard the phone ringing. I ran as fast as I could to answer it.

"Johnston residence."

"Zuria, it's your cousin Lucinda."

"Oh, hello." She was not the person I expected on the other end of the line; my disappointment must have been obvious.

"Hello to you too? What am I, chopped liver or something?" Lucinda jokingly asked, but with a hint of irritation.

"No, of course not. I'm just waiting for an important phone call. What's up?"

I knew why this gold digging bitch was calling. The only time she ever called me was when she needed money. I barely knew her; she was my third cousin on my mother's side. Ever since she found out she had a cousin with a little dough set aside, she'd tried a number of times to be new best friends.

"I just wanted to see how you were doing...that's all. Did you hear about Manuel?" Lucinda asked.

"I'm fine, thanks. Yeah, I heard about him," I said, answering her questions abruptly, without giving her much more to work with in the conversation.

She was always in Manuel's face, friendly but flirting, when she came to visit me.

Eventually, I got fed up and told her that he was off limits. That wiped the smile off her face and finally got her to sit her hot ass down somewhere.

"Send my condolences. I hope he gets well soon," she said.

I took a moment to scream at her, but only in silence. She loved wasting my time. Didn't she have a player's ball to go to or something?

"Oh, Lu, I heard a beep. I have to answer this call," I said quickly. The caller ID said it was Amir.

"Wait! I need to ask you something."

"Ask me another day. Really sorry; I have to go."

I thought I handled that quite well. What I wanted to say was, "Bitch, ask me in a letter! Don't call my house anymore!"

I clicked over to Amir's call without saying goodbye.

I was so glad that Amir interrupted that meaningless conversation. I had never trusted her, probably because she reminded me so much of Manuel...selfish and vindictive. Hell, I should've introduced those two to each other a long time ago. That gold-digging whore probably would have been thrilled to have his baby!

"Hello. Hello?" I said impatiently, still somewhat frustrated at the previous call. I quickly reminded myself of who I was talking to.

"What's up, Zuria? It's Amir."

"It's about time you called me," I said playfully as a smile split my face from ear to ear.

"Oh Z, I only got in an hour ago. I really had to unpack and take a hot shower. Traveling always wears me out, but now, I'm feelin' fresh! How's your day going?"

"Better now that I'm talking to you. Have you eaten, yet?"

"Not really. I had a few bags of gourmet peanuts on the plane; that was all I could keep down. It was a tiny little plane; it sounded like it was falling apart as we were flying."

"My poor baby! Maybe I can make you feel better. Do you want any company?"

"That would be very nice; I've been looking forward to it since I left."

"I'll pick up some Lo Mein on the way, alright?"

"Perfect. I'll be waiting, impatiently!"

"See you soon."

"Ciao, bella."

***

I rehearsed my confession/explanation while I ordered the food, walked along the sidewalk and drove in my car. I was clearly distracted, because a few people honked at me. Apparently, I was taking my sweet time driving under the speed limit, delaying the inevitable as much as I could. I was about to have one of the most serious discussions of my life; it wouldn't be easy. It usually only took me twenty minutes to reach Amir's place, but I decided to take the business route this time, and intentionally get caught in traffic.

The closer I got to his flat, the more I started to panic. I circled the block twice before I finally pulled into his driveway. He had a beautiful home, a perfect two-bedroom bachelor pad. He didn't have enough room for a bunch of children playing in the yard, but it was spacious enough for him.

I looked at myself in the rearview mirror, then realized that my foot was still on the brake pedal and that the car was still running. I really needed to fix my face, before I rang the doorbell. I didn't look great, as though I'd taken a few months off from normal sleep. Amir must've heard me pull up, because I could see him peeking out of the window, waving at me.

I hid my makeup kit and waved back. I said one more prayer; it couldn't hurt.

Amir greeted me with a brilliant smile and kissed me so long and hard that I almost lost my grip on the Chinese food. He was wearing nothing but a bath towel wrapped around his waist. As he walked towards the bedroom, he called back over his shoulder, telling me to make myself at home. I took a seat at his dinette table and unpacked the lo mein. It always impressed me how immaculate he kept his apartment; it sparkled with cleanliness but also had a cozy, broken in feel.

I kept my mind on what I had to tell him. But, in a final excuse to myself, I decided to wait until after we had eaten and discussed his trip. *God, I don't want to have this conversation*, I thought.

"Go ahead and start without me," he yelled from the back room.

"I'll wait, it's plenty hot."

He came back fully dressed, holding a large bag, a crooked grin plastered on his face. I looked inside and saw a pair of gold designer shoes, a sleeveless red, lace dress and assorted pieces of gold costume jewelry.

"For my queen!" Amir said proudly, beaming.

"Oh, Amir! You shouldn't have, sweetie," I said gleefully.

"I want my best girl to always look her best."

I held onto my smile, but inside, I felt a stab of pain. I had to tell him or I wouldn't be able to relax. *Or maybe, I could hide it for a while. He doesn't have to know about it now, right? No, Zuria...grow up!*

My mind was racing with conflicting ideas. I had always been an honest person; I didn't want to start lying to the man I loved.

He noticed the sudden change in my mood and seemed concerned. I wasn't doing a very good job of hiding the fact that something was on my mind.

"Z, what's wrong?"

I paused; he could read me so easily, the best and worst part of intimacy between two people. "Amir, I don't know what to say. You've been so wonderful to me. But I have something to tell you, and I don't know how you're going to take it," I said, trembling in nervous anticipation.

I sat at the dinette table, feeling numb. I held back the tears as long as I could, but Amir already looked frightened. He sat down across from me and silently waited for me to continue. I looked across the room, considering a final flight to freedom through the front door. No, I needed to get this off my chest now; the secret was consuming me.

"I'm not sure where to start. A lot has happened since you left. First of all, Manuel was in a car accident and is still in critical condition. I went to visit him and I was overwhelmed, I had never seen him so broken. While the doctor gave me all the details of his condition, I got flushed and fainted."

Before Amir could say anything, I held up my hand to stop him, and began to feel the tears running from my eyes.

"After admitting me, they did a standard checkup and found something. Apparently...I'm...I'm pregnant" I said, and burst out into a fresh wave of tears.

I could see the thoughts scrambling through his head, rushing at full speed in countless directions.

"Pregnant...well, wow. Is it mine?"

I leaped up and began walking towards the door to freedom. He followed me into the hallway, and as I attempted to open the door, Amir reached out and closed it. I could feel his body behind me, but I couldn't bear to look him in the eye.

"I can't do this anymore, Amir. I think I should just do you a favor and leave."

"Z, stop. Please. Have you been sleeping with someone else?"

He looked calm and there was no anger in his eyes. Yet, I couldn't believe what I was hearing.

"Of course not, Amir. I would never do that to you. I'm in love with you; I need you to know that. This all happened before we spent that night together...while I was still with Manuel."

I sobbed blindly like a child who has lost her favorite security blanket.

Amir is in disbelief, but he turned me to face him and pressed my head to his chest. My tears soaked into his shirt almost immediately, and for a moment, all I could think of was that he had just put on a clean shirt and I was ruining it. He allowed me to cry as long as I wanted to. At some point, I felt his chest heaving with sobs as well.

"What are you going to do, Zuria?"

"I want to keep the baby. I'll raise it alone, I don't want anything to do with him." There was a pause.

Amir was such a rational and cool person, despite the poetic, emotional side of his personality. His mind immediately began working again, once his emotional outburst had subsided. "Do you think he'll give away his rights? What if he wants custody of the baby?"

"I don't want Manuel to ever set eyes on this baby, let alone have rights to it. He won't have any choice but to give away his rights. He's not fit to be anyone's father."

"Come here, Z...sit down by the fireplace; you're trembling."

We sat down and stared into each other's eyes, holding hands.

"I'll be by your side as long as you want me there," he said softly.

"I was so afraid to tell you. I just found out about it, so please don't think that I've been keeping it from you all this time. I wanted to tell you as soon as you got back, but I couldn't do it over the phone."

"I believe you, Zuria. Don't worry about that."

I dried my tears on my sleeve, but they threatened to fall again at any time.

"Amir, I can't expect you to help me raise a child."

"Listen...we'll just take it one step at a time. I'll help you get through this."

"How can you be so understanding? And say the perfect thing every time?"

"My mother taught me three things; not to judge anyone, not to take life for granted and to always respect myself. And she said that those go double for women," he said with a grin.

"Your mother sounds like a wise lady. I wish I could have met her."

"She'd have loved you. She's probably looking down right now, but if she were here, she'd say, 'Stick by this woman...she's a good one'," Amir said, imitating his mother.

"You really don't know how much you've changed my idea of men. I came close to giving up when I left Manuel. You've opened my eyes to so many things I didn't understand. You taught me to give love, and earn it. It's funny, I finally discover that some men can be kind, gentle, and compassionate, and now the only man I want is right in front of me."

"Zuria, just let me know if you need anything; I'll do whatever it takes to make it happen." He looked like he was holding something back. I remained quiet, as he had with me, to give him his own chance to open. "I have something to tell you."

"I can tell. What's wrong, Amir?"

"I...I...I've been keeping this from you for a while now. It is difficult to even say it out loud."

"What is it?" I asked anxiously, my emotions preparing for one more plunge on the same rollercoaster I'd been on for days.

"I want you to know..." He paused and took a long, deep breath. "I see you as wife material, that's all."

"What? Really?"

"Seriously, Z. I don't mean now, just...maybe, one day when the time is right."

My heart felt full to bursting, so I gave him a little peck on the lips. He responded by climbing on top of me, kissing and biting on my neck. I couldn't believe how painless that 5-minute discussion had been.

"Now, let's eat before the food gets cold," he said.

"Chinese food doesn't get cold for at least an hour or two," I said jokingly.

We laughed. We ate our food and talked delicately about the baby and how both of us would have to cope with the inevitable changes. It felt awkward discussing it so maturely, after two days of gnawing fear and anxiety on my part. However, that's why Amir was the man I loved, rather than the true father of the child growing in my stomach. I didn't want to press on too many issues, or discuss it so much that he might have second thoughts, but I felt the bricks of stress and worry slowly dropping off my back with each passing minute. Life was far from perfect, this situation was less than ideal, but I began to believe that we would handle it as well as anyone.

Chapter 15

Amir was standing in the ICU, looking slightly uncertain. He walked into Manuel's room carrying a bouquet of daisies. He set the bouquet on the bedside table loudly, startling Manuel out of his sleep.

"What's up?" Amir said, grinning.

Manuel's eyes looked like they were about to burst from his sockets.

Amir grabbed a chair, sat down on it backwards, and folded his arms across the back, staring intently at the tubes, hardware, and machines that surrounded Manuel.

"Looks like you've gotten yourself all fucked up, man!" Manuel watched Amir's every move, and made high-pitched noises from his throat, as if cursing him in guttural Spanish.

"What was that? I must have missed it."

Amir paused as he examined Manuel's badly bruised and broken body.

"I know you're probably wondering why I'm here, and why I brought you the daisies. Well, it's sort of symbolic; you'll figure it out eventually. The thing is, I've been thinking about you, amigo. I've realized that you aren't really that tough after all. I mean, any man who likes to beat on a woman is nothing but a batty boy...and a fucking coward."

Amir looked behind him to see if anyone was coming. His tone was cold and clear; he didn't want Manuel to miss a single word.

"You see, I'm gonna tell Zuria about my past, and she'll forgive me for keeping it from her for so long. I'm not the bad guy here. You on the other hand, are a blackmailing, mind-fucking, woman beater," Amir said as he bit his lip. His calm demeanor was cracking as the blood began to boil behind his words.

Manuel was sweating profusely. He was also mumbling hysterically.

"Oh, and by the way, you won't be seeing Zuria again. I'm going to ask her to marry me. She'll accept my proposal, because I'm a real man that can commit to something he loves. Don't bother contacting her ever again," Amir said as he shrugged his shoulders. He had come to say what he wanted, and it felt good.

A nurse came in to check on Manuel. The nurse looked at Amir strangely as he stood up from the chair. Amir smiled and decided that it was probably best to go. Manuel's mumbling had gotten louder.

"We're old friends," Amir told the nurse.

The nurse tried to calm Manuel down and told Amir, "Okay, but he seems quite agitated. Maybe you should go, maybe come back another time."

"Yes ma'am," he said obediently.

Amir stood beside the bed and patted Manuel on the leg, which was almost fully encased in a cast. He flashed Manuel a concerned glance, knowing that the nurse was looking at him, then smiled at her once again.

"No pasa nada. I'll take care of Zuria and the baby until you get well...okay, amigo?"

He looked at the nurse a final time, winked and walked to the door with a grin on his face. In the doorway, he paused for a moment, and then turned around.

"I hope you like the daisies."

Chapter 16

Chase knocked twice on the door, then came in anyways, bringing in two big bags of assorted stuff for my newborn baby. There was no need for a baby shower, since Amir and I had basically bought an entire store's worth of stuff over the past few months. Despite that fact, Chase was always finding more shit to add to the baby's room.

"Oh, she's such a beautiful little thing!" Chase said as he took her out of my arms.

"Do I get a kiss?" I asked, feeling a bit jealous.

"Of course you do, honey!"

"Do you want another pillow for your back, baby?" Amir asked.

"The first fifty pillows you gave me are working just fine, love," I responded, gently teasing him.

I smiled and patted him on his arm to let him know how much I appreciated his concern. He had done more than anyone could have ever imagined over those past six months. I just wanted him to sit his ass down next to me and relax.

Chase took a seat on the sofa. He rearranged the baby's clothes and swaddled her in her blanket.

"So, Mama...have you been taking your pain meds?" he asked.

"Sweetie, you know I don't like taking pills. I never have; besides, I'm breastfeeding," I said obstinately.

"The doctor said that the meds are fine and won't hurt the baby, but Zuria still won't take them," Amir explained calmly.

"Sure, the doctors say that today, but five years from now, they'll be on some commercial explaining how harmful they are. Then where would I be?"

"Amen, girl!" Chase agreed.

The doorbell rang, and Amir got up to answer it. I heard the mailman's voice and Amir exchanging friendly banter for a moment. I stared at the large, brown box as Amir brought it over to me. *It must be for the baby.* There was no return address on it, which is pretty unusual, especially for a big delivery. I paused for a few seconds, considering what it could be, and from whom. Chase startled me out of my own thoughts.

"Open it, Zuria!" Chase urged, clearly excited. He loved presents, even when they weren't for him.

Slowly, I cut the tape on the edges and opened the box. It was a large stuffed animal Pooh Bear. I searched for a note beneath the fuzzy form, or at least a card. There was no indication of who sent such a thoughtful gift.

"Who's it from, Z?" Amir asked.

"No idea. I'm still looking for a card," I replied.

The box was definitely empty. I searched for some explanation in my mind instead.

"It could be from a co-worker, or maybe a few of them got together and bought it. I'll call Susan about it later," I said.

"Well, she is a bit of an air head; she probably forgot to write an address," Chase chuckled as he laid the baby down in her bassinet.

We watched her squirm as Amir stood over her, tickling her tiny feet.

He was so good with her, and I quietly thanked God, like I did every day, that things were working out between Amir and I. He'd been staying the night with me, ever since I had Nyima, but he hadn't "moved in" exactly. I just needed someone to help out, since I couldn't move around much because of the stitches. The delivery hadn't gone as smoothly as I had expected.

I looked over at her and smiled, my little Nyima Jade Johnston. She was 7lbs 6oz when they finally brought her into the world. She had a light, honey-colored complexion with brown curly hair and long legs. Everyone said that she took a lot after her mother, but I see the facial features of her father as well, especially in her eyes. She also had Manuel's temper, so when she was hungry, the whole neighborhood would know! I just hoped that the similarities would stop there, and that she wouldn't get worse. Seeing Manuel in her eyes was okay, seeing him in her heart would be difficult to bear.

Despite my feelings about Manuel's impact on Nyima, she was beginning her life with an amazing example of manhood; I don't know what I would do without Amir. He had been cooking intriguing, delicious meals almost every night. He had never cooked more than twice a week for himself, so he was no gourmet chef, but he's a naturally creative person who loves to cook for others, and I love to eat, so I'd always end up being his guinea pig. I'm also not that hard to please! His vegetarian dishes were always impressive and I melted every time I smelled his chocolate brownies baking in the oven.

***

After Chase left and his bag of gifts had been opened and put away, I went into the nursery to check on Nyima. The Pooh Bear was sitting in the corner looking alive, smiling crookedly at the opposite wall. I took a seat in the rocking chair and wondered who could have sent the bear. I called Susan, who said that she hadn't sent it. My family and friends had brought presents when they came to visit. I was in mid-rock when I figured it out. I didn't know how I hadn't thought of it sooner.

I had heard through the Atlanta gossip grapevine that Manuel was out of the hospital. His mother was taking care of him while he went to the doctor for daily physical therapy. Although I didn't totally understand the whole condition, he apparently had an incomplete spinal injury, which gave him some hope of walking again. Word on the street was that he'd been healing at an almost miraculous rate. The injury hadn't changed his attitude much; a girlfriend of mine heard that he'd shoved his mother against a wall for trying to help him eat his food. His upper body strength clearly hadn't gone away, nor had his anger issues. I just wanted him to stay away from Nyima and me. I had left that evil behind me, and that was where I wanted to keep it.

I was sitting in the kitchen, thinking about my stuffed animal revelation when Amir arrived with a gym bag full of clean clothes and other necessities. He was always running errands for Nyima and me so I didn't have to leave the apartment. He closed the door with his foot and set the bags on top of the kitchen island.

"Are you feeling okay?" Amir asked.

"Sure, never better," I said, still sulking around the living room.

"Is that sarcasm I'm hearing, lady?"

"No, no, no...I actually am feeling a bit better. I've been moving around more today."

Amir continued to put away the groceries.

"Is Nyima awake?" he asked.

"Not yet. She's been sound asleep since you left. She'll be awake and begging for another feeding soon enough," I said. The idea of that reminded me of how drained I felt, and not only of my nutrients.

"Has anyone called today?"

"Not yet. I guess most people have gotten the hint that I'm done with the phone calls and the visitors. If someone else asks about the baby one more time, I'm going to lose it!"

I joined Amir in the kitchen to help him put away the groceries, but he led me straight back to the sofa. I appreciated the generosity, but even that had its limits, so I insisted on helping him. He got a kick out of me rolling my eyes and sticking out my tongue at him like a petulant child, but he didn't object to me putting away the groceries while he put dinner in the oven. We walked back together to the sofa and collapsed; both of us were exhausted for different reasons.

"So, did you ever find out who sent the bear?" he asked.

"I think so, yeah," I said. I didn't want to upset him, so I tried to change the subject casually. "Did you see anyone at the market?" I asked.

"No. Who sent the bear, luv?" Amir said, a slight edge to his voice.

I really had to work on my ability to change the subject. Amir was too smart for that sort of thing.

"Well, I mean...I'm not positive, but I can't think of any other explanation...Manuel must have sent the bear," I mumbled.

Amir said nothing, but immediately stood up and headed for the phone book. I saw a flash of his face as he stood up; he looked furious. I was terrified.

"Amir, what are you doing? Please, there's no reason to do anything. I don't even know if he sent it. It's not worth getting upset over!"

"That piece of trash must have bumped his head even harder than I thought, Zuria! If he comes near you or Nyima, I'll put him back in the hospital, or I'll put him in the ground!" Amir said flatly. His eyes were seething, but his voice was even, calculating, and cold.

"Amir, stop it! You're scaring me. Let this go!"

He stood in front of me a different man, volatile and powerful. Mainly, I could see that he would do anything to protect me from my past.

He had a white-knuckle grip on the phone book, but I laid my hands over his and felt them relax. I took it out of his hands, and never tore my eyes away from his. I could see his chest slow, and the blood rushed out of his face. His anger drained out of him, and I swallowed my saliva hard.

I took a step back and tried for a second time to change the subject.

"Dinner is almost ready, why don't you go wash your hands. I've been craving some of that delicious, baked fish pie all day," I said as I rubbed his back and guided him into the hallway.

"What, so now you like the fish pie?"

"I love your cooking! I love it almost as much as I love you!"

"Such a sweet talker...thanks Z," he laughed.

He wrapped his arms around me before he went into the bathroom to wash his hands. It had scared me to see him so angry, but simultaneously safe because I knew how fiercely he would fight for me. All I had left to worry about was telling him that I truly hated fish pie. That could wait for another day.

***

I woke up in the middle of the night to Amir moaning, tossing, and turning. He was having a nightmare and talking in his sleep; I couldn't help but listen. I don't know why; there was something intimate and secret in listening to someone speaking while they're sleeping. Unfortunately, after a few moments, I could tell that it wasn't anything I wanted to hear. I was afraid to wake him up, in case he started swinging. I sat up and watched him carefully. Suddenly, he cried out like a frightened child. I gave him a shake or two to try and bring him out of it.

"Amir, wake up, sweetie. It's Zuria! I'm here," I said, stuttering and shaking in fear. I turned on the lights, so he could see where he was, and who he was with. His eyes were wild; he looked terrified as he sat up in bed. Sweat was pouring down his face and arms, and I noticed that his side of the bed was soaked through with perspiration.

"Wait here, baby. I'll get you some cold water," I said as I threw back the sheets and put on my robe and slippers.

I ran to the fridge and poured a tall glass of water. On my way back to the bedroom, I grabbed some fresh towels and bedroom sheets from the linen closet. I poured a little of the cold water on a hand towel and placed it on his forehead. I handed him the glass, and he took small sips from it, but kept staring at some distant point that I couldn't see, lost in the terror of his nightmare.

"Amir, drink this, you're safe," I said softly. His eyes refocused on me, and he seemed to be calming down as he came back to reality. I had never seen him so distraught, or seemingly out of control. "Tell me what happened, Amir."

His expression raced from anger to sadness to fear before he answered me. "It was just an awful dream. From when I was little," he panted. He took a deep breath and wiped away the tears roughly with the back of his hand. "When I was young, I used to hide under my bed when my stepfather started beating on my mom. My mother always tried to protect me from him, so if he raised his hand at me, she'd step in and take the brunt of his anger. I hated him, before I even knew what hate was, but mostly, I was just afraid. I never wanted to come home after school because I didn't know what kind of mood he'd be in."

I stroked his head in silence and gave him a few more sips of water.

"Well, one day I came home from school and my mother was in the kitchen cooking dinner. She kissed me on my forehead and told me to go to my room, so she and my father could finish talking. Her words didn't make it seem like anything bad was going to happen, but I felt a hard lump in my throat and my stomach got tight, like I was going to be sick," Amir choked out as he fought to hold back the tears building in his eyes.

Then, Amir began to sob uncontrollably. I pressed his head to my shoulder and pressed my lips into his hair.

"Take your time," I whispered into his ear.

"Then, I heard a thump. And another. I came out and found my stepfather standing over my mother, beating her with his belt. I ran to their bedroom and locked the door, then called the police. I begged them to come save my mother. I ran back to the kitchen to try and stop him. Mum sounded like she was choking on something and when I got back to the kitchen, he had his belt strapped around her neck. I had to do something quick, so I started pounding on his back with my fists, trying to distract him, or take the beating instead, as my mother had always done for me. He turned around and punched me in the stomach. I fell against the wall and cracked my head; I remember feeling the blood run down the back of my neck."

Amir's eyes were glazed over, completely lost in the terror of his memory. He took the glass from me and began to drink the rest of the water. He looked at me with bloodshot eyes, tears still threatening, and continued to confess his oldest, darkest secret.

"I ran to their closet and got my stepfather's pistol. I had found it there when I was playing hide and seek a few years earlier. I didn't even think; I just ran into the living room and shot him in the back. He fell to the floor and I ran to my mother and took the belt off her neck. But she was dead. So was he."

I couldn't believe what I was hearing, and I felt like I was going into shock. My heart sank deep into my chest, and I walked to the nearby window and raised it so I could gasp for fresh air. The wind could've picked up my lifeless body and blew me away. Amir fell to his knees by my side, as I stood leaning against the windowsill, frozen in the midst of the cool breeze.

Amir reached up and put my hand in his, and when I looked down, he was gazing intently at me, waiting to speak.

"Zuria, I didn't want to keep it from you. I tried to tell you the day that you came by my place to tell me about the baby. I didn't know what you would think of me. I was only a child, but one that killed his stepfather. I spent a decent amount of my childhood getting evaluated by psychiatrists and doctors. It took me a long time to realize that I wasn't an evil person, just a child who didn't know how to protect his mother."

"Amir, I can't possibly imagine what you went through, and that's a part of your past that will never fully disappear. No matter how the situation played out, it still involved two people that you loved dearly. I hear horrendous stories every day at work, I mean, my job is to help children and their families get through tough times. Sometimes, I check on those kids on my days off, because I'm afraid of what might have happened before Monday morning. As much as I care about them, I know that the memories will never disappear for them either."

I pulled back a few of his flyaway locks; he wears them tied back at night. He held his face in his hands. I knelt down next to him and pulled him into me, cradling him in my arms. We sat there, silently contemplating what the next day would bring. I didn't want anything to tear us apart, and I knew that I could help him with his pain, as he'd helped me with mine. Whether he would help me break down the walls that he'd built was the real question; only time would tell.

Chapter 17

I was strolling with Nyima through the park on a beautiful afternoon, about a month after Amir had his nightmare breakdown. Summer was coming to a close and the pleasantly cool breeze was a sign that fall had arrived. Amir and I officially moved in together, and he put a ring on my finger. He decided to sell his place and move in with me, since I had more space. My home was paid for as a gift from my parents, so bills would never be much of a problem. Our goal was to invest in more stocks and bonds and set up a trust fund for Nyima's college education. Amir had been trying to persuade me to move away from here and start over. But, I wasn't ready yet...maybe in another year or two.

Nyima was happy, and she was a quiet, well-behaved baby; she took after her mother in that respect. Looking into her eager, innocent eyes, I felt as thrilled as a kid in a candy store. I looked down at my diamond engagement ring that sparkled in the sunlight. I checked myself out from head to toe; I had never felt so content in my life. I had finally found a real man who cherished me and worshipped the ground I walked on. I couldn't ask for anything more.

After walking through the park a few times, I decided to sit on a bench and enjoy the beautiful day. Nyima was asleep, so it was a rare and perfect time to read a magazine and soak up the sun. I had always been easily drawn to those romance and relationship magazines, especially the ones that included the ten ways to please a man. I always wondered who wrote that shit; at least Amir and I never had to worry about having a boring sex life. We were incredibly creative in that department!

I searched through the colorful pages, looking for any particularly juicy gossip. It seemed like those damn celebrities couldn't stay married for more than a day. Maybe they were just too busy to add someone else into their hectic schedule, let alone the most intimate parts of their lives. Or maybe they were simply too focused on their beautiful bodies, money and fame. Some people care so much about their lover's appearance; they treat them like trophies just to look good in the public eye. Unfortunately, deep within their self-absorbed world, they are never alone, yet always lonely. It's not hard to lust. However, it is hard to commit. Figuring out why that was true was one of the greatest challenges in life.

I allowed all of my senses to relax, and in the silence of my mind, I was keenly aware of my surroundings as I continued reading the magazine.

I smelled the aroma of freshly baked bread from across the street; it made my mouth water and my stomach moan. I had a few sips of my lemon green tea to quench my thirst and suppress the hunger pangs that were climbing. I touched the hand-woven baby blanket that Nyima lay under to let her know that her mama was still nearby.

Out of nowhere, I heard loud, pounding bass coming from a car cruising through the park. The Reggaeton music made me want to dance, but I snapped my fingers and rolled my head instead, dropping some attitude that I hadn't shown in a long time. I kept my head stuck in the magazine, but the volume of the music lowered as the vehicle stopped about five feet in front of me. Instantly, my womanly intuition kicked into gear, and my heart began to race. I didn't even take the time to question it; my gut was telling me to get up, grab Nyima and leave the park.

I closed my book and placed it in the diaper bag.

I looked up cautiously, trying not to be too obvious, and saw Manuel staring at me from the car with disappointment and barely concealed rage. His dark, mean eyes couldn't deceive me. It was the same look he used to get right before he landed a blow across my face or moments before knocking a guy's teeth out for looking at me from across the bar.

He sat on the passenger side, restrained behind the safety belt for the moment, at least. Then, he began to slowly shake his head and suck his teeth in that cruel, trashy way of his. I had never seen the driver before in my life; the white Infiniti they were in must be his ride. I looked at Nyima, who lay sleeping by my side; I wished she was already in my arms, and that we were walking away. I didn't bother to move; I almost forgot to breathe.

"Hey there, Zuria. How's life treatin' ya?" Manuel asked.

"Very well, thanks. And you?" I replied.

"Well, it could be a lot worse, ya know."

"I agree. If life gives you lemons, you'd better make some lemonade."

Manuel took a few seconds to laugh aloud, longer than the moderately funny joke really called for. He stopped abruptly, then fixated his sly eyes on the stroller as he lowered his tone.

"Who do you have there?"

I paused, unsure of where this conversation was going. "Her name is Nyima Jade," I said, as I turned my head to take a peek at my little princess.

I watched Manuel from the corner of my eye. He had a toothy, hungry grin on his face.

"So, when were you going to tell me?" he asked.

"What? I have nothing to tell you," I said.

"When were you going to tell me that *my* baby was growing inside you while I was on my back in the hospital?"

"Frankly, I figured you wouldn't give a damn if I did!" I said fiercely.

The emotions of fear, anger and resentment were starting to rise in me again; I could feel my heart pounding in my chest.

"Why are you letting that muthafucka help you raise *my* little girl, Zuria? Damn it, I'm the father! You can't do this to me!" Manuel said in one breath, a strange mix of desperation and anger were battling in his voice.

"Please, calm down. You're scaring Nyima," I said softly as I gently rocked the stroller, hoping that she would continue to sleep. I looked down to see the baby squirming and frowning, as if she was debating whether to cry.

"Answer me, you slut!" Manuel shrieked.

I grabbed the rest of my things and the stroller. I started walking quickly in the opposite direction, not saying another word. I heard a car door open and slam, but I didn't want to look back. Instead, I reached in my purse to find my cell phone. My fingers were fumbling for those three digits, 911, when I felt something warm dripping down my white, cotton t-shirt. The pressure of something violently fast and strong threw me forward. The stroller broke loose from my hands and I heard my phone shatter when it hit the pavement. I stumbled forward, but was reaching for the stroller instead of breaking my fall. My head cracked with a sickening thud into the pavement and everything went black.

I felt the fresh, cool breeze that I had come to the park to enjoy. I heard the noise of sirens getting closer, and the hummingbirds still singing their endless tune in the trees above me. I was lying underneath a very tall woman. My vision was quite blurry and my head was racked with spasms of sharp pain, so I couldn't see her face clearly. She seemed to be as tall as the pine tree standing motionless behind her. She was holding my baby, or was she an angel with wings made of light? I couldn't hear Nyima crying anymore. My vision closed in like a fade out in a movie; I could only hear the sirens, the hummingbirds, and the thumping of blood in my ears.

My body was getting cold, and I shivered from head to toe. I couldn't move. The fear began to surge in my chest, and I could no longer feel the warmth of the sun shining between those still pine trees.

Everything else had ceased to exist, except for the beautiful hair on the lady standing above me and the hummingbirds staring down at me with their wretched eyes. In rolling waves, I could hear the sound of the fresh, cool breeze delicately blowing in my ear, along with the sirens that continued to approach. I couldn't tell which direction they were coming from, but I prayed that they were nearby.

As the vehicle approached, the silhouette of the woman and the baby vanished from my narrow field of vision. Had my eyes been deceiving me? Suddenly, I felt a gentle touch on my shoulder. I heard the dull murmur of a crowd that had begun to form around me.

I heard a voice from far away, pulling me out of the deep well of darkness; "Hello, ma'am? Can you hear me? Please, stay calm. I have to cut your shirt so I can see where the bleeding is coming from."

I was in a daze, but the shock was beginning to wear off. I gasped and felt excruciating, burning pain on my whole right side, starting at my shoulder and flowing down to my fingers, which felt as though they were on fire.

"What's happening? Where's my baby?" I asked frantically. I tried to move and roll onto my left side.

"Ma'am, you've been shot, please lie still. I need to find out where the bullet hit you. Your baby is fine. She's with my friend over there," said the man, apparently a paramedic.

It took all of my strength to focus my vision and see Nyima being bundled up by a short, dark haired woman in a paramedic uniform. She smiled at me as she lightly patted Nyima on the back.

"Ma'am...what's your name?" the paramedic asked.

"Zuria...Johnston," I said faintly.

"Well, Miss Johnston...it looks like you're going to be fine. You were hit in your right arm. You're a very lucky woman! This might have been much worse if the witness hadn't surprised your attacker and chased him off," he said.

"Where is she? I want to thank her," I said, my vision was swimming again; perhaps I was moving around too much, I had probably lost a lot of blood.

"Miss Johnston, it was a he. The witness is a young man just getting off work and walking across the park to get home," the Paramedic said, slightly confused.

I scanned the surrounding area, trying desperately to focus as I looked around the park. It was relatively empty, except for the witness who saw the incident, and the small group of people who had come to see the sirens. There was no tall woman, nor was there an angel strolling the paths with wings made of light. My "hero" was talking to the police a few feet away, occasionally glancing over at me, still concerned for my safety.

***

There I was again, in that cold hospital bed, just like the place where my sister had writhed and moaned in agony until the day she died.

I could see Amir and Chase talking in the hallway. They both looked exhausted and upset. All I could see were furious facial expressions being traded back and forth. I looked down at myself to see what condition I was in. My arm was wrapped in bandages, but other than that, I didn't see any problems. My head was still fuzzy and ached fiercely, and I remembered happily accepting the painkillers from Dr. Walters earlier that day before fading back out of consciousness. It was a good thing that I pumped and froze enough milk for the baby; I had a feeling that I'd be slamming pain meds for a while. I felt like I was floating on a cloud. Those pills were no joke.

I felt a light touch on my leg; Dr. Walters was in the room again. "Miss Johnston, press this button if you need anything, okay? You're safe here, just get some rest, alright?" he said, patting me on my right knee.

"Okay, doc. Is that really all you do in the hospital? Get some rest? Shit...*rest* should be free!" I giggled.

Dr. Walters smiled, nodded his head and left the room. I kept giggling as he walked away; he had a funny walk. He was pretty weird, but sort of cute! I shook my head to clear out the laughter, remembering that the two most important men in my life were outside, clearly not laughing.

I looked out the door and saw my best friend and fiancé still talking in heated tones. I could tell that Chase had been crying and he was shaking his head in disbelief. Amir had a hypnotized, emotionless expression plastered on his face. He punched one hand slowly into the other as he talked, accentuating certain things he was saying. I tried to read his lips, but they were moving too fast. All I could think about was Amir's temper, which only seemed to show itself when Manuel was the subject. If he went after Manuel, he would get hurt, or worse. Obviously, I didn't want him to go to jail for hurting Manuel, either. I wanted to grab his hands and kiss his anger away. We had to let the authorities take care of this now. As my mother always told me, "Vengeance is mine, saith the Lord!" Somehow, I doubted that Amir was going to be easily swayed.

Finally, Chase and Amir walked into the room. Chase hugged me carefully, and kissed my cheek. He was careful not to touch my arm, as though it was going to break off at the slightest bump. Amir sat on the bed and just held my hand, saying nothing. I could tell that they were trying to stay strong and calm for my sake, but their body language said it all.

"We know everything that happened, so you don't have to say a word," Chase said.

Another wave of powerfully shivering drugs flooded into my head again, and the calming effect was like a warm blanket wrapping up my brain. I couldn't have been serious even if I'd wanted to.

"I shouldn't have let you go out alone, Zuria. I'm so sorry!" Amir said as he squeezed my hand.

"Amir, don't be silly. You can't protect me all the time. It's not your job to stand in front of bullets for me," I said.

"But you know I would. In a heartbeat," Amir said. Tears were slowly running down his face.

"They've arrested Manuel and his friend, Carlos. Carlos is the son of a bitch that shot you. I'd love to get my hands on both of them! What piece of worthless trash would shoot an innocent woman, especially when her baby is sitting two feet away in a stroller?" Chase said, clearly infuriated.

"Someone must be watching over them, because if I had gotten to them before the police..." Amir said, trailing off before he could finish his thought. Chase and I both knew what he was probably going to say.

"Amir, let's all be rational here, okay? Just let the police handle them. Don't get involved," I pleaded.

"You're a hell of a woman, Z. I'd be going after them too. But maybe she's right, Amir," Chase said.

I could sense that Amir had been slowly filling with anger and frustration while I was carrying Nyima, because he knew that eventually, something would have to be done about her father. He told me about his visit to Manuel in the hospital and that we might have to face Manuel again.

I had simply tried to pretend that Manuel wasn't alive, so I could raise the baby with Amir. Unfortunately, wishing something were true doesn't necessarily make it so. I had a gunshot wound on my arm to prove it.

"I have had something to tell you for a long time, but I didn't want you to worry, so I kept it to myself. I honestly didn't think that Manuel would take it this far," Amir said as he wiped at his eyes, as though preparing for tears that weren't there yet.

"Amir, what is it? What did you do?" I asked.

"I'll let you two have some privacy," Chase said.

"No! Please, stay," I insisted as I stared at Amir from head to toe. I honestly didn't know if I could take any more dramatic revelations or tragic news.

Amir continued his story, but was clearly choosing his words carefully.

"It's actually what I didn't do that makes this so fucked up! I met Manuel Cartagena right before you two broke up. One night, he was waiting for me outside of Sage's Jazz Café. He had seen you and I together, talking and laughing, and assumed that you were cheating on him. He told me to stay away from you, or I'd regret it. We argued a bit, and I walked away."

Amir paused and dropped his head in shame. I knew that wasn't the end of the story, so I sat up and shook my head to clear out the fuzz of the drugs. I didn't want to miss a single word.

"He told me that he knew about my past...about when I shot my stepfather. He tried to blackmail me, Z. He even offered me money to leave you alone. I didn't think you would believe my story over his, so I agreed to leave you alone. But, I never took his damn money!"

He gently smacked the bottom of his right hand into the palm of his left and continued. "At the beginning, I thought about leaving you alone, because I didn't want to get involved in some messy lover's quarrel.

But, as I got to know you better, I fell for you, hard. Baby, I've never met any woman more real than you. Obviously, I was worried about Manuel saying something, but I decided that although my past was bad, my future would be worse if it wasn't with you."

"Damn, Amir this is too much! Why didn't you tell me? What were you thinking?"

"I didn't want to lose you, or lose the love I have for you...the love we have for each other. I couldn't let some clown take that away! If I had told you about my past when we met, would you have been able to look at me the same way?"

I took a brief moment to consider the question, and then answered confidently and honestly.

"Well, I would've had a lot of questions for you."

"I thought you would've just seen me as some fucked up basket case. You're too classy to ever actually be with some emotionally unstable kid. You have such a big heart, and I thought you might just feel sorry for me, which would have hurt just as much. I couldn't tell you everything at once, Z. I'm so sorry for keeping all of this from you; it's been killing me."

"Amir, everyone goes through darkness in their life. It doesn't matter where you're from, what race you are, or how much money you have. No one has a perfect life from start to finish. I can't imagine the pain you must have felt growing up, or how that changed you into the man you are, but yes, you should've told me everything! I'm a big girl...I could have handled it."

"You really are one hell of a woman. I'll never keep anything else from you, baby. I promise." Amir reached out to wrap his arms around me; I could see the gratitude and the love shining in his eyes.

Chase stood frozen by the wall, his eyes flooded with tears. I had actually forgotten that he was in the room. He seemed to come alive when we turned our focus to him.

"This is better than a damn soap opera! Honey, I won't ever need to go to the movies again. Not when I can get you two for free!" he joked.

We laughed and hugged each other tight. I was glad that Chase was there. I had a daughter, and a wonderful man, and Chase seemed to fill out my growing "family" in the perfect way.

It was impossible for me to be upset with Amir. I understood that what he'd done, or not done, had been because of how he felt about me. He couldn't have known how cruel and manipulative Manuel could truly be. I certainly couldn't blame him for not predicting the insanity of Manuel's behavior. Honestly, I was just happy that he and Chase were there for me, as I knew they always would be.

Chapter 18

I sat on the floor in my daughter's room, reading about her biological father in the paper. When she got older, I knew that I would have to explain to her that her real father is in prison for the attempted murder of her mother – me. Although I felt no pity for Manuel, and was glad that he was out of our lives forever, it made me sad to think about someone growing up with that knowledge about their own father. I wanted her to know the truth before she discovered it in some other way, but when that time was exactly...who knows? For now, Amir is her daddy, and that's all she needs to know.

The newspaper stated in undeniable black and white: "*Manuel Cartagena and Carlos Alvarez have been found guilty of the attempted murder and malicious wounding of Zuria Johnston. They will spend a life sentence in the state penitentiary with the possibility of parole.*"

The idea of him getting parole made me slightly sick to my stomach; I wanted him to spend the rest of his days there. Fortunately, Manuel can never keep his mouth shut for very long and loves a good fight; he wouldn't be getting out anytime soon.

***

It had been a month since Manuel's sentencing, and when I saw him through the reinforced glass of the prison, his eyes almost looked remorseful. He told me that he would always love me. I told him that he needed help, because his brain was clearly twisted. He seemed to have a rehearsed speech about feeling bad for putting our baby in danger and for being angry enough to try and kill me. I was hearing him, but I refused to actually listen to a damn thing. I'd been down that road of manipulation and deceit before, and that was before his friend had put a bullet through me.

He was lucky that a window was between us. If it weren't for that, I would have liked to reach over and smack him across the face. After all those years of him pushing me around, it was almost good to think about his role as fresh meat in prison. I'm sure there would be plenty of people to smack him around inside.

At least I had closure; I had intended to tell Manuel goodbye for a final time.

"I hate you for what you've done, and for the man that you've become. You should be ashamed of yourself. At least you'll have the rest of your life in this hole to think about it," I said, as calmly as possible. I didn't want him to get a final rise out of me.

"Well, I hope you find it in your heart to forgive me, someday, sweet...tender...Ayanna," Manuel said, looking straight into my eyes, challenging me with words that weren't his.

That was what Amir called me...sweet, tender Ayanna! I had no idea how the hell Manuel could have known that. He must have been following us all this time. Hell, given Manuel's track record, he probably bugged my house.

I didn't give him the satisfaction of getting upset and storming out, or making a scene. He always wanted me to lose my cool, because at that point, he was able to manipulate me, or break me down and make me feel so small. My life had changed over the past year, and I had become a different person. His games no longer worked on me, yet he really believed that he could still pull the strings and make me dance.

"Who's the caged bird, now?" I asked intensely, powerfully holding his gaze until he was finally forced to look away.

He was speechless for once in his life. I thought I could almost see tears in his eyes, but I didn't need the proof of my victory; I knew that I had won. I took one final look at him locked in his cage where he belonged, and I boldly stood up and exited the room.

Some people may have thought that I was crazy for going to see him. Perhaps they don't understand why I needed to so desperately. For several years, Manuel had been trying to erase the person I was. During our relationship he attempted to do it mentally and emotionally, then he tried to physically eliminate me with a bullet in an empty park. I needed to show Manuel that he had failed in all of his attempts. I didn't need him, and I would never need him again. I had found true love and there wasn't a soul on earth that could break that bond. Manuel had lost; I was free.

Chapter 19

My wounds were healed and I was getting ready for the most important day of my life. My mother and Chase were helping me get dressed; my father and the others were outside talking loudly as usual, celebrating the day. That was the first day of the rest of my life, when I turned over a whole new leaf. Within minutes, I would be Mrs. Zuria Townsend. My heart was beating so fast that I could practically see my chest twitching in the mirror.

My makeup, hair and jewelry were finished, all compliments of Chase. I was dressed in a spectacular gown of white lace, embroidered with patterns of flowers. I chose not to wear a train; I didn't want to trip and embarrass myself in front of everyone I knew on my wedding day.

Lastly, Chase put on my veil to complete my newly beautified appearance. I looked in the mirror; *Black women look good in white!* I thought to myself. When I looked back at Chase, I finally had a moment of clarity. This was happening. It had all worked out.

We gave each other hugs and air kisses so he wouldn't smear the makeup that he'd put on me. I fanned my eyes to keep back the tears.

"Zuria stop being a baby! This is a happy day, the happiest day I've had since I first met you," my mother said, stubbornly holding back her own tears.

"Today is the happiest day! These are tears of joy!" I said.

We happily stood in our positions and the music began to play. My mother held my hand until it was time. I looked up at the sky and thanked God for everything over the past year, especially this perfect day. I also thanked my sister, Nadia, for being there with me when I needed her most. She was the tall woman I saw in the park with a baby, my niece, in her arms. I knew that I would always have angels around when I needed them. I knew they were both watching as I heard the music begin to play.

The door opened to the backyard of our new home in St. Thomas, Virgin Islands. It was full of beautifully decorated tables and a crowd of even more beautifully dressed people. My father came to stand beside me, proudly beaming at the assembled guests. I wrapped my quivering arm around his strong one; he's been the wind beneath my wings all of my life. Chase and his partner are standing in front of us with Amir. A sweet, soulful voice singing, "Heaven," sent chills down my spine. It was the perfect song for the angelic theme my mother and I had chosen for the wedding.

My family and friends were all there to support us, and a destination wedding also makes for a good excuse for a vacation. I watched everyone else walk down the aisle; it seemed like a very long walk. My moment of clarity returned as I realized that after the unbelievable journey I had taken to get there, I was only a dozen steps away from embracing happiness and making my dreams a reality. It was a walk to heaven, although I had been through hell to get there. Amen. I walked out slowly and the crowd turned as one to greet me, smiling and snapping photos.

Amir stood tall in his sharp black and white tuxedo, a solid red silk tie, and patent leather gators. I was so blessed to have a man that would go to extremes to prove his love and protect it. We needed one another to keep the other person strong, motivated, and loved. He vowed to never put his hands on me the way Manuel had done. He said that if he was going to touch me, he'd rather have it be with kisses. I believed every word. I knew that I was his savior and that he was mine.

When I reached the front, and was facing Amir, I had a flash of memory back to the poem that I performed at Sage's Jazz Café when Amir and I first connected. When I laid my eyes on his dreamy, adoring gaze on our wedding day, some of those verses floated back into my head. From that moment on stage, I knew that Amir was who my life was meant to be spent with.

"This feels so right. Perfect. After all this time, I can't believe that it's finally here. This dream is real!" I said to Amir, moments before we began the ceremony.

"It was *real* from the very first day we met, Ayanna. There was never any other choice for us," he replied.

"My love for him is real and it keeps on getting stronger. His touch whispers secrets to my most secret spots. And, like empty bellies, they wail out in hunger. The taste of his lips is sweet. Divine. His smell is fresh like rain and summer wine. Damn, he's so fine! From this day forward I'll give one hundred percent; fifty isn't enough when my heart knows he's God sent."

###

www.ingramcontent.com/pod-product-compliance
Lightning Source LLC
Chambersburg PA
CBHW070455130626
46555CB00003B/1007